FIRSTBORN SONS

PROFILE

FIRSTBORN SON:	Jack "Flash" Dalton
AGE:	32
STATS:	6'2"; short, dark hair; slate-blue eyes; lean and hard
OCCUPATION:	Former U.S. Navy Seal
AREA OF EXPERTISE:	Surveillance photography; hand-to-hand combat
PERSONALITY:	A battered knight with rusty manners
FAVORITE SPORT:	Exploring underwater wrecks
MOST CHARMING CHARACTERISTIC:	The ability to give any mission—or woman—his full attention
BRAVEST ACT OF COURAGE:	He and his team did six courageous things every morning before breakfast. But the toughest thing he ever had to do was walk away from his job.
PREFERRED ROMANTIC SETTING:	A cold beer in a warm bar always suited him just fine. So why do moonlit nights on a Montana mountain suddenly have so much appeal?
GREATEST PASSION:	Making the ice princess lose her cool...

Dear Reader,

There's so much great reading in store for you this month that it's hard to know where to begin, but I'll start with bestselling author and reader favorite Fiona Brand. She's back with another of her irresistible Alpha heroes in *Marrying McCabe*. There's something about those Aussie men that a reader just can't resist—and heroine Roma Lombard is in the same boat when she meets Ben McCabe. He's got trouble—and passion—written all over him.

Our FIRSTBORN SONS continuity continues with *Born To Protect,* by Virginia Kantra. Follow ex-Navy SEAL Jack Dalton to Montana, where his princess (and I mean that literally) awaits. A new book by Ingrid Weaver is always a treat, so save some reading time for *Fugitive Hearts,* a perfect mix of suspense and romance. Round out the month with new novels by Linda Castillo, who offers *A Hero To Hold* (and trust me, you'll definitely want to hold this guy!); Barbara Ankrum, who proves the truth of her title, *This Perfect Stranger;* and Vickie Taylor, with *The Renegade Steals a Lady* (and also, I promise, your heart).

And if that weren't enough excitement for one month, don't forget to enter our Silhouette Makes You a Star contest. Details are in every book.

Enjoy!

Leslie J. Wainger
Executive Senior Editor

Please address questions and book requests to:
Silhouette Reader Service
U.S.: 3010 Walden Ave., P.O. Box 1325, Buffalo, NY 14269
Canadian: P.O. Box 609, Fort Erie, Ont. L2A 5X3

BORN
TO
PROTECT
Virginia
Kantra

Silhouette®

INTIMATE MOMENTS™

Published by Silhouette Books

America's Publisher of Contemporary Romance

Special thanks and acknowledgment are given
to Virginia Kantra for her contribution
to the FIRSTBORN SONS series.

To Suzanne Brockmann and Candace Irvin, sisters in arms.

And to Michael, always and forever my hero.

Special thanks to OSM, for giving my fictional princess a real research
question; to Dr. Kathy and Franzi Zabolitski, for giving Jack an
honest-to-goodness injury; and to Pam Baustian and Judith Stanton,
for reasons too numerous to mention.

 SILHOUETTE BOOKS

ISBN 0-373-27170-0

BORN TO PROTECT

Printed in U.S.A.

Bound by the legacy of their fathers, six Firstborn Sons are about to discover the stuff true heroes—and true love—are made of....

Jack Dalton: He takes his job of protecting pampered princess Christina Sebastiani *very* seriously. But nothing in the rule book prepared this battered warrior on the proper code of conduct to follow when the headstrong virgin tempted him at every turn!

Princess Christina Sebastiani: The last thing she needed was a well-muscled bodyguard with a take-charge attitude distracting her from her research. *Especially* a sexy ex-navy SEAL who awakened her every feminine desire...

Major Jonathan Dalton: The natural leader of the "Noble Men," he has a secret agenda when it comes to his disillusioned son.

Princess Julia Sebastiani: Although she is tucked away in an ivory tower in Montebello, Julia and her unborn child could be in grave danger....

Sheik Ahmed Kamal: He swears that he is innocent of the crimes against the royal Sebastiani clan. So if Kamal's to be believed, who *is* responsible for these cold-blooded acts of terrorism?

A note from award-winning writer Virginia Kantra,
author of six Silhouette books:

Dear Reader,

Once upon a time…

The first story I wrote—I was nine, I think—began that
way. The first stories I loved, about brave warriors and
proud princesses and unexpected danger, all did, too. So
when I got the call from Silhouette to write my very own
fairy tale, in Intimate Moments' FIRSTBORN SONS
continuity series, I jumped at the chance.

Being invited to participate in a series that features some
of my favorite authors was another big plus. It's been a
joy coordinating stories and bad guys with them.

This story was meaningful to me in other ways, too.
Fathers and sons fascinate me. I have two wonderful sons
of my own, themes and variations of their father. And my
husband, like the hero of this book, is a firstborn son
whose father served in Vietnam.

Of course, my warrior is the modern sort—a U.S. Navy
SEAL. And my princess is a microbiologist—or, as she
would be quick to correct you, a microbial ecologist—at
Montana University. But the themes of love and honor
and courage and characters who aren't quite what they
appear to be are timeless.

I hope you enjoy this story of a princess who learns her
own worth and a battered warrior who discovers the
magic power of love.

Love,

Virginia Kantra

Chapter 1

Jack Dalton hitched his seabag up on his shoulder. His uninjured shoulder, the one that wouldn't let him down. On the elevator door in front of him, some college banana with more sense of humor than respect for university property had slapped a bumper sticker: Montana, the Last, Best Place...to Hide.

Jack's mouth quirked. Funny. And fitting. Not that Jack was hiding, whatever the old man accused him of. Drifting, maybe, but not hiding.

He prowled toward the stairs. The habits of physical conditioning were hard to break. And even the navy docs admitted there was nothing wrong with his legs. He could still climb to the lab before the elevator descended to the science building lobby. He could still run six miles in thirty-nine minutes or less. He could still stand for three hours in fifty-degree seawater without dropping or complaining.

What he couldn't do anymore was swim.

What he couldn't be anymore was a U.S. Navy SEAL. Life was a bitch sometimes.

The ugly concrete stairwell caught every echo and threw it up and down. There was access onto each floor, through the basement and, he guessed, out onto the roof. He'd made only a cursory check of the building. He wasn't playing at point man. No one was relying on him anymore to spot bad guys and booby traps.

He hiked quickly and quietly up the stairs. Lots of stairs. His seabag rubbed the banister. A line from one of his sister's bedtime stories came back to him: "Once upon a time, a princess lived in a tower...."

Jack shook his head. Kid stuff. Unfortunately, the woman at the top of these steps was no fairy tale. Christina Sebastiani of Montebello might have fled the palace for life among the books and Bunsen burners, but there was no getting around the fact that she was a real live princess. Montana University was an accredited ivory tower.

And the danger... If his father could be believed, that was real, too.

It was just her highness's tough luck that Jack was no knight in shining armor.

He exited the stairs and stalked the hall, counting doorways out of habit, noting angles from windows. Security sucked. Any thug with a gun and an agenda could have this floor pinned down in minutes. Not his problem, Jack reminded himself. He was only passing through.

A black plaque on the door identified the biology lab. A pane of frosted glass obscured his view of the room. Silently, he turned the knob and slipped inside.

This was the place, all right. He did a quick scan of shelves packed with bottles, and long black islands cluttered with glassware. Silhouetted against the painted cinder block, with two Bunsen burners flaring and a couple dozen petri dishes laid out before her, stood a single, slender figure in a white lab coat. Female. Blond. His hormones sat up and took notice. Now *that* was a complication he didn't need. But it had been a while, a long while, since he'd had a woman under him.

She was a research scientist, his father had said during their brief, tense phone conversation. Jack had immediately pictured some dumpy, frumpy little woman in plastic goggles with her hair piled haphazardly on top of her head.

The goggles were there, pulled down around her neck. The hair was swept back smoothly from her face and caught in a clip. And her face... He sucked in a breath Her face had the cool, don't-touch-me perfection of a portrait under glass.

This was Princess Christina Sebastiani of Montebello? Damn.

As he watched, she jiggled open the top of a glass bottle with the tip of her pinkie finger and held it to the flame. The intensity in her eyes—blue?—and the soft absorption of her mouth made his hands itch for his camera.

He wondered why he hadn't seen her photo splashed on the tabloids in the checkout line. She was as much a looker as the rest of the Sebastianis—the only royal to inherit the queen's blond beauty. But judging from the media coverage, her older sister, Julia, was the princess in the public eye, her younger sister, Anna, the one with the public's heart.

He waited while she poured stuff from the bottle into a petri dish, swirled it around and closed the container tightly. No point in making her spill. She recapped the bottle, and he let his bag slide to the floor with a soft thump.

Christina jumped. Straightening her shoulders, she

glared at him. Yeah, those eyes were blue, all right. Cool blue and hostile.

"You must be lost," she said. "The bus station is across from the stadium."

Jack admired her swift recovery. He even kind of liked her snotty tone. "I know. I just left there."

She looked him over. He knew what she saw: a big man in his early thirties, his convalescent pallor overlaid by a three-week tan and a day-old beard. His military haircut had mostly grown out. His jeans were creased with travel, his leather flight jacket powdered with dust. Not a reassuring sight for any woman working alone on an almost empty floor, let alone a princess.

"Then can I help you?" she asked.

He raised one eyebrow. "What did you have in mind?"

Her full lips pressed together. In annoyance? Or fear? "You obviously don't belong here. If you don't leave, I'll have to call security."

"Maybe I am security," he suggested, just to see what she'd do.

"You're not in uniform. And I don't see a university ID tag."

She was cautious. That was in her favor. She was gorgeous. That was in his. For the first time, Jack began to think maybe he wasn't crazy for listening to his old man's suggestion that he drop in on the exiled princess of Montebello.

"I don't work for the university," he said.

Her eyes narrowed suspiciously. "Did my father send you?"

Jack considered awarding her another point for swiftness and then decided against it. It didn't take a rocket scientist to figure out that after the recent attack on his eldest daughter, Julia, King Marcus would want to protect his family. His entire family. Including emancipated Christina.

"Not your father. Mine. He's a..." Now, how the hell was Jack supposed to describe Jonathan Dalton? Decorated war hero. Mercenary soldier. Texas tycoon. Consultant to kings, and lousy dad. "...a friend of your father's," he finished lamely. "He knew I was going to be in the area and asked me to look you up."

"Really?" Christina's tone was dismissive. Disbelieving. "And who is your father, exactly?"

"Jonathan Dalton."

Her blue eyes widened. "*Uncle* Jonathan?"

Jack felt poleaxed—whether from the impact of that suddenly warm blue gaze or the notion of the old man as anybody's benevolent uncle, he really couldn't say. "You must have him mixed up with somebody else. Jonathan Dalton," he repeated. "Thick white hair, little white beard, tall—"

"Yes," she said impatiently. "I remember. He used to give Anna candy. And he taught our brother, Lucas, how to fieldstrip and fire a gun."

It was more than Major Dalton had ever done with his own children. Hell. Jack had never liked trading on his father's influence. But just talking about the guy had brought a sparkle to the princess's eyes, a lilt to her voice.

He rubbed his jaw. "You see a lot of him growing up?"

"Not a lot. I know he and his friends fought side by side with my father during the rebellion."

That fit. Jack had heard those stories, too, about the young king of Montebello and the band of renegades and heroes who had served with Jonathan Dalton in Vietnam.

More fairy tales, he figured. His dad never did anything without an eye to the almighty dollar.

"Yeah, well, they're back in touch," he said.

Princess Christina nodded. "Because of the threat from Tamir," she said. "Father always said he could trust Uncle Jonathan."

"Oh, he trusts him," Jack agreed. "In fact, this time he's trusting him into supplying you with a bodyguard."

The princess angled her chin, her eyes speculative. "You?"

"Me," Jack confirmed.

"No," she said flatly.

The major had told him to expect a refusal. Princess Cupcake here had resisted all the palace's earlier attempts to provide her with protection. But Jack still felt a lick of irritation. Maybe he wasn't the type to inspire confidence in a pampered royal, but he was good at what he did, damn it. *Had* been good at what he did. Had been the *best*.

"Relax. I haven't agreed to take the job yet."

"Then why are you here?"

"Recon," he answered. No SEAL team undertook a mission without assembling a target folder.

He was no longer a SEAL.

He heard the crack as she set down the glass bottle she still held in her hands. "You're checking me out?" Her voice was ice over outrage.

He shrugged. "Your father wants you protected twenty-four-seven. It's only reasonable to see if we can stand each other long enough for me to get the job done."

Christina gave him a frosty look. His stupid body reacted as if a bar girl in Bolivia had just given him the eye. Definitely, he'd been out of action too long.

"Very well," the princess said. "Now that we've established that we can't, as you say, stand each other, you can refuse your father's money with a clear conscience."

But that was the problem. Jack couldn't. Not until Christina had some understanding of exactly how much danger she was in. Not until he did. No matter how little he relished playing baby-sitter, no matter how satisfying it would be to tell the major to go to hell, no matter how often Jack told himself he wasn't a warrior anymore, his own stubborn need to protect wouldn't let him walk away from a situation. He at least needed to report to the old man that the princess was working long hours alone with no security.

Frustrated, he stuck his hands deep in his pockets. "Forget the money. Look at where things stand. You've got your older brother missing and presumed dead. You've got bombs going off in your homeland. You've got some sheik guy—"

She crossed her arms across her shielding white lab coat. "Ahmed Kamal of Tamir."

"Whatever. Some Sheik Kamal trying to claim the kingdom and kidnap your big sister, and your parents are worried sick about you. Don't you think you ought to take some precautions?"

She lifted her eyebrows. "I have taken precautions. I live in Montana."

Her dry tone, her unexpected humor, slipped under his guard like a knife. He rubbed his jaw with the back of one hand to wipe off his answering grin. "Your father doesn't think that's good enough."

Christina sighed. "Mr. Dalton, my parents don't think anything is good enough for their children. I honor them for that. I love them. But I am not going to sacrifice my privacy, compromise my focus and interrupt my work by accepting the services of a completely unnecessary bodyguard. I assure you, I am quite safe here. No one can find me."

Despite his frustration, he liked the aloof, precise way she had of speaking. Not that he accepted for one minute what she was saying, but she sounded really smart. "I found you," he pointed out.

"I'm sure you had directions."

"So will Kamal's men."

"Assuming I'm a target. I have only your word for that. And I don't even know you. For all I know, *you* could be working for Sheik Ahmed."

Jack regarded her grimly. "Are you always this pissy?"

Her lips curved. "I've been told so. Yes."

He had a sudden urge to back her up against the counter and bite into that regal, smiling mouth. Hell. He really had been out of action too long. He fished in his back pocket for his wallet, ignoring the slight pull in his shoulder, and tossed his identification onto the table. His gaze dared her to pick it up.

After a moment's hesitation, she did. Cautious, he thought again, with approval. She looked first at his Texas driver's license and then at the white plastic card issued by the Department of Veterans Affairs.

Her brows drew together. "'Senior Chief'? You are U.S. military?"

"Former military. Navy SEAL, retired." Forced out, he thought. He for damn sure hadn't quit. Navy SEALs weren't quitters.

"You are young to be retired."

Bitterness flooded his mouth. "Medical retirement," he said evenly.

"Ah." The soft sound could have signaled anything. Acceptance. Pity. Dismissal.

Jack hated all three.

"I can still function, your highness," he snapped.

She regarded him steadily. He wondered how much of his rage and desperation he'd given away by that one stupid remark.

"I wasn't questioning your qualifications, Senior Chief," she said quietly. "You are obviously able to protect me. Assuming I needed your protection, which I do not."

"Your father thinks you do."

"My father is a warm and sentimental man who is still grieving the loss of his only son. It is natural for him to overreact."

"Yeah? Well, my father is a cold and calculating son of a bitch who wouldn't waste time or manpower on a dead-end assignment. If he says you need a keeper, then you do."

Christina recoiled. No one talked to her that way. No one. Her heart was beating way too fast. She felt threatened—by his warning, yes, but even more by his attitude. She was a Sebastiani. She did not need this hard, unshaved stranger to remind her of the world she'd left behind. She did not want him invading her sanctuary.

She met his gaze and almost shuddered at the raw energy that burned in those bitter blue eyes. She should not have to deal with this. She was woefully unequipped to deal with *him.*

And she could never let him know.

Years of training supported her head and stiffened her spine. "Mr. Dalton, I have made a life and a career quite separate from my family. It is highly unlikely that terrorists are traveling across nine thousand miles and ten time zones to kidnap an inconsequential member of the royal house of Montebello."

His jaw set. Even through her agitation and the shadow of darkening beard, she noticed it was a very nicely squared jaw.

"And what if you're wrong?" he demanded. "You're

not inconsequential to your father. What if Kamal decides to use you for leverage in this land dispute?''

''I am not without friends—or defenses. This is Montana. Strangers are noticed here.''

''Nobody noticed me. Or stopped me.''

No one would dare, she thought. He looked dangerous. Alien. His tough, lean physique was more than a match for most university types, even the outdoorsy breed attracted to field sciences in Montana.

And she had no excuse for inspecting his physique. Her cheeks grew warm.

She turned off the gas burners before the combination of their heat and her inattention set fire to the lab. ''Perhaps they noticed and decided not to say anything. The other benefit to living in Montana is that people here tend to mind their own business. And if you would go back to yours, I could continue with mine.''

It was a nice line. She was proud of it. Unfortunately, he was less impressed.

He stuck his thumbs through the belt loops of his jeans, the pose emphasizing his blatant masculinity. ''What if I decide to make you my business? What are you going to do about it?''

''I have no idea,'' she admitted frankly. ''You're too big to ignore. If you are also too rude to leave, I suppose I would call my father and tell him to have you dismissed.''

''Do all the men in your life do what you tell them to, princess?''

There were no other men in her life.

A royal princess—even an ''inconsequential'' one from a tiny island kingdom like Montebello—had to be careful if she wanted to keep her name and picture out of the tabloids. Christina had long ago accepted that meant no

dance club dates or midnight walks or tender dawn part-
ings that could be captured by a telephoto lens. Since coming to America, she had tentatively tried to take part in the
safer aspects of university life. But her rank excluded her
from the grad students' beer-and-pizza parties, and her age
made her an oddity at the faculty's wine-and-cheese mix-
ers.

And so she was careful, and safe, and alone.

None of which was any of his business.

She lifted her brows and said, in her mother's most regal
tone, "If they're smart, they do."

He nearly smiled, and the heat in her cheeks climbed
several degrees. "I must not be very smart then," he
drawled. "Because I just may stick around."

Dumb, Dalton. Very dumb.

He did not want to work for the major. Princess Cupcake
had made it more than clear that she did not want him
working for her.

But even as he acknowledged his mistake, Jack punched
a number into the motel phone. He listened to the ring,
stretching his legs over the ratty print spread on the room's
one double bed. So it was a dive. To a guy who'd stayed
in huts in Colombia and tents in Kuwait, these were luxury
accommodations.

A woman answered the phone. In the background, Jack
could hear a baby fretting. "Hello?"

He settled back against the squeaky headboard, trying
to ease his injured shoulder. "Hey, Janey," he said.

"Jack?" Warmth suffused his sister's voice. "Jack, how
are you? Where are you? Daddy's been trying to get in
touch with you."

"I'm in Montana. I'm looking into doing a job for
him."

"Oh, Jack." Real worry vibrated down the line. The major's "jobs" had hung over their childhood like storm clouds on the Texas horizon. Jack had shrugged and shouldered the job of man of the house, first accepting and later welcoming their father's frequent absences from home. But Janey was different, he thought with affection. Janey believed in home and family, had married young and borne her adoring husband two kids already. "Is it dangerous?"

"Hell, no. He just wants me to baby-sit." Jack wouldn't give her details that could endanger her, and she wouldn't ask. They had both grown up with that, too.

"Well, you're a good baby-sitter," his little sister said. She added, "He said to tell you he had a package for you. If you wanted it."

And by leaving word with Janey, the old man had neatly deprived Jack of the chance to turn him down. Smart, Jack acknowledged. "Fine. Tell him to send it. I got a post office box today." He gave her the number.

"Jack…" Janey's voice was soft and hesitant. "Are you sure you want to take orders from the major?"

He didn't resent her asking. She'd witnessed enough battles growing up to know the likelihood of combat. "It beats a desk-puke job, Janey. It beats doing nothing. And the lady I'm assigned to has a body worth guarding."

"Oh, well, then…" He could almost hear her smile. She was cheered, as he knew she would be, by the thought of her big, bad brother falling for some home-and-hearth skirt. He didn't disillusion her. "As long as you know what you're getting into."

"That's me," he said, working hard to keep the bleakness out of his voice. "Always prepared. Now that I've washed out of the SEALs, maybe I can become an Eagle Scout."

* * *

The department secretary ripped a sheet off her pink message pad and slapped it onto a stack.

"Dr. Sebastiani isn't in the lab today," she said.

Jack knew that. The lab had been empty. He'd come to the biology office to find her.

"Does she have a class?" he asked.

"No."

"Office hours?"

The secretary, a young woman whose short dark hair and long silver earrings emphasized her Native American features, regarded him impassively. "Not on Tuesdays."

Okay. Jack was beginning to appreciate Christina's reliance on her Montana neighbors. As a first line of defense, the biology secretary was remarkably hard to shift. But she was no match for a terrorist with an AK-47. Or a SEAL with a mission.

Abruptly he switched tactics, offering the young woman his hand and his best smile. "Sorry to make such a pest of myself. I'm Jack Dalton," he said, as if the name would be familiar to her.

She blinked. Blushed. And reached cautiously across her desk to take his hand.

"I still don't know Chris's schedule very well," Jack said sheepishly, giving her hand a little squeeze before releasing it. "But we had kind of a misunderstanding last night, and I was hoping I could catch her. To apologize."

"Oh." The young woman's eyes brightened, as he'd hoped they would, at the prospect of a romance. But she still didn't roll over completely. "Have you two known each other long?"

"Our families go back forever." Jack sat on a corner of her desk, broadcasting clean-cut reassurance, glad he'd taken the time to shave that morning. "But you know how it is with these long-distance relationships. The last couple years have been tough. I mean, she's here, and I've been—'' he checked himself, as if recalling the need for discretion ''—overseas,'' he finished with another smile.

This time the secretary smiled back. ''I can see how that would be difficult. I'm sorry you missed her.''

Jack shrugged. ''That's okay. Do you know when she's expected back?''

''It's hard to say.'' The woman adjusted the silver eagle pendant around her neck, showing it and her cleavage off to their best advantage. ''Dr. Lyman called in sick today, and Dr. Sebastiani agreed to take her tour down to Bald Head Creek. Those things can go on all day.''

Jack felt a lurch of unwelcome fury, of unfamiliar fear. Christina had chosen to go out in public. Unprotected. A potential kidnapping target, with nothing to defend her but a bunch of scientists and her own snooty attitude.

''Guess I'll do my groveling later then,'' he said easily, and stood. ''Thanks for your help.''

''No problem,'' the secretary said. She lowered her voice confidingly. ''I hope you two can work things out. She's a really nice lady.''

Jack managed not to snarl. *Nice* was not a word he was tempted to apply to Princess Tall, Cool and In Control. But he didn't have to stay and argue. He didn't have to do anything but find her.

''Oh, we'll work something out,'' he said.

Or he would be forced to tie her up and sit on her while he figured out what to do next.

Chapter 2

Bald Head Creek glittered like a promise between banks canopied by cottonwood and lush with long grass. The winding water reflected glimpses of wide, blue Montana sky.

So beautiful, Christina thought, breathing deeply of the damp, cool air. More beautiful than anything but home. Regret brushed her. She ignored it.

"Everyone have their counting trays?" she called cheerfully.

The eighth grade science class from Meriwether Lewis Middle School, assembled on the banks around her, nodded and waved shallow plastic trays in response.

"Let's go hunting then," Christina said, and dipped her net into the stream bed.

Water sparkled as she scooped up her load and swung it toward the bank.

A girl in a blue sweater scrambled away from the dripping net of creek muck. "Eeeww!"

Other thirteen-year-olds crowded closer as Christina emptied her catch, mud and pebbles and creepy crawlies, into her collection bucket.

"Cool."

"Gross."

"Yuck."

"What's that?"

Smiling, she ladled samples into the students' collection trays, describing what they were likely to see, explaining how to identify and count the tiny aquatic insects and record their finds on their clipboards. Downstream, she had another student team measuring water temperature. Later, they would calculate the creek's flow using a stopwatch and a stick.

Like Pooh and Piglet, she thought fancifully, racing twigs from the bridge in the Hundred Acre Wood. A.A. Milne's classic was one of her mother's favorites. The Queen, a former governess, had always taken the time and care to read to her own children at bedtime. Christina remembered snuggling with her sisters while her brother, Lucas, lounged male and superior in the doorway.

Christina cleared her suddenly constricted throat and focused, as she always focused, on the work. On work and on the bright, interested faces of the students bending toward her as she knelt on the muddy bank.

"All right now." She plunged her hand into the muck, winning groans and giggles from her audience. "This little fellow here…" Gently, she separated out a caddis worm with her thumb. "Can anyone tell me what he's called?"

She wasn't sure at what exact moment she felt the change, like a rise of temperature in the air around her. Like the kiss of a branch on the back of her neck. Like the glide of the sun on her cheek. As the students scattered with their counting trays, she rinsed her hands in the cold stream. Under the splash and calls of the children, she heard the whisper of her own breath.

She stood slowly, her gaze scanning the opposite bank. Nothing.

She paused to correct a clipboard entry and stop the girl in the blue sweater from tipping the contents of her collection tray down a boy's back.

And when Christina straightened, when she turned to check on the other group of students taking water temperatures downstream, she saw Jack Dalton standing above her on the bank.

For a moment she couldn't think, move, breathe. She froze like a doe in a hunter's sights as he stood watching her, lean and tough and out of place in his light T-shirt and leather jacket. His face was hard. His eyes were slate-blue and unreadable.

Her blood drummed in her ears. And then her mother's training kicked in. *Chin up. Eyes straight.* She drew a shallow, careful breath. *You are a Sebastiani.*

"You frightened me," she said with dignity.

"Good." He came down the bank, his boots slipping slightly on the wet gravel. "You should be frightened. What the hell are you doing out here?"

She raised her chin another notch. "Conducting a field trip on riparian ecology and the importance of the watershed."

From downstream, she heard a couple of yells, a yelp and a splash.

Fascinated, she watched as a corner of Dalton's hard mouth kicked upward. "And here I thought you were under attack," he said.

She smiled back reluctantly. "That may come later. Excuse me, I'd better go see what's going on."

He fell into step beside her. "I can tell you what's going

on. Somebody got pushed into the water. And you shouldn't be out here alone, miles from town, miles from the university.''

She resented him setting limits on her activities. If she'd wanted to live by palace rules, she would have stayed in Montebello. If she could have stomached the constant scrutiny, she would have stayed at UCLA.

''Hardly alone, Mr. Dalton. I am surrounded by thirteen-year-olds.''

''Yeah, and they'd be big protection if Kamal's guys decided to snatch you now, wouldn't they? If you won't think about your safety, you should think about theirs.''

Her mouth firmed. ''I am thinking of theirs. Dr. Lyman was ill, and someone needed to come down here with the class. I assure you, the students are at greater risk of drowning than I am of being kidnapped.''

They rounded a bend in the stream and saw one of her charges floundering knee-deep in icy water while his friends laughed on the bank.

''Eric Hunter!''

The laughter subsided into fits and sniggers.

Eric looked up warily, all freckles and false innocence. ''Yes, ma'am?''

Christina swallowed a bubble of amusement. ''Get out of that water this instant.''

''I can't.'' He sounded pained. ''My sneaker slipped, and I'm stuck. My ankle.''

She frowned. She hoped it was only stuck. The boy could walk the half mile back to the bus in wet shoes, but not with a sprained ankle.

''All right,'' she said, unzipping her nylon field jacket, preparing to wade in after him. ''Stand as still as you—''

But before the words were out of her mouth, Jack Dalton

was in the stream. Pushing his sleeves back to his elbows, he bent down.

"Put your hand on my shoulder," he ordered.

The boy's mouth dropped open. Christina suspected hers did, too.

"For balance," Jack explained, plunging his arms into the water. "Your hand on my shoulder. Now."

Tentatively, Eric obeyed.

"Okay, your sneaker's wedged under this rock," Jack said calmly. "I'm going to shift it, and I want you to pull your foot out. Got it? On three. One, two, three."

Christina glimpsed Jack's mask of concentration and the boy's hand clutching the brown leather of his jacket. The clear, dark water surged and splashed. And then Eric, supported by Jack's arm, staggered out of the stream and collapsed onto the bank.

"Let's take a look," Jack said.

But Christina was already kneeling, the gravel sharp and cold through her twill slacks. She was picking at the boy's sodden laces when she noticed the water streaming from Jack's boots. His jeans were soaked to the knee.

She looked up ruefully. "You got wet. I'm sorry."

"This isn't wet. You should have seen me in BUD/S." Her face must have betrayed her lack of comprehension, because he grinned sharply. Her breath caught. He really was most attractive when he smiled.

"SEALs training. Basic Underwater Demolition," he explained.

Christina nodded, still not really understanding. "Can you wiggle your foot?" she asked Eric.

"He won't have a fracture," Jack said as the boy moved his foot cautiously from side to side. "Ligament will give before bone."

"Which means what?" Christina asked, pushing down

the wet, sagging sock. She pressed her lips together. The ankle was already puffy.

"If the ligaments are stretched, it's a strain. Partly torn, it's a sprain. Either way, all you can do is elevate the ankle and ice it."

"I don't have ice."

"Did the kids pack lunches?"

She frowned. "I—yes, I believe so."

"We put our drinks in coolers," Eric volunteered, leaning back on his hands. "Ow. There's ice in the coolers."

Jack shrugged. "There you go, then."

"The coolers are on the bus." She sat back on her heels, looking up at him. "I can't leave the children unsupervised. Could you…?"

"Sorry. I can't leave you unsupervised, either."

Her pleasure at his quick, practical response vanished. "I am not thirteen, Mr. Dalton. I am well able to take care of myself."

"That's what you think. You two." The boys still on the bank straightened abruptly. "Can you find your way back to the bus?"

They looked at him. At each other. Back at him. They were little boys, Christina thought. Not soldiers. But as instinctively as any palace flunky, they responded to his tone of command.

"I guess."

"Sure."

"Do it, then. Take one of those tray things and bring back ice."

"It's half a mile to the parking lot," Christina objected. "Besides, they're responsible for measuring—"

"They're responsible for seeing that their buddy is all right after landing him on the rocks. Go on, now," Jack ordered, and they went, crashing and sliding along the trail.

Christina drew a tight breath. She would not be dictated to like one of the children. "We should move Eric up the bank. And raise his foot."

"Right," Jack said, surprising her by his cooperation. "I'll take care of it. You do the teacher stuff. Measuring, was it?"

"Temperature and current flow," she confirmed. She studied Eric, his freckles stark in his pale face. Uncertainty fluttered in her stomach. He was her responsibility. Should she cancel the field trip now?

"We'll be okay," Jack said quietly. "I'll keep cold water on the ankle till the kids get back with the ice. Is there something this guy can do in the meantime? You got another of those clipboards?"

Christina seized the idea thankfully. Activity would distract Eric from his discomfort and make the wait easier. "He can record times for the rest of the class when they measure currents. I'll go wrap up the water life project, and bring the kids here."

"Don't be gone long," Dalton warned.

Irritation pricked her. Outdoors in Montana, she didn't need anyone to tell her what to do. This was her place, her area of expertise, and no fish-out-of-water seaman with blue eyes and big muscles was going to order her around.

Still, she was obliged to him. She stifled a sigh. Queen Gwendolyn had instilled in all her children a very strong sense of their obligations.

"I'll be back as soon as I can," she said, and made her escape.

She was as good as her word, Jack thought.

Christina strode back within five minutes, her charges strung out behind her like a bunch of baby ducks, wading and wobbling off course. And instead of doing her princess-in-a-tower routine, all distant and aloof, she laughed and listened and encouraged them, and splintered his perceptions. Again.

He'd been wrong about her. Once upon a time that kind of misjudgment could have gotten him killed. Now it got him interested.

There were grass stains on the knees of those fancy catalog pants and a streak of mud on her cheek. Her eyes were bright. Her face was flushed, and she smiled often. She looked like one of the damn kids.

And then, in response to the slowly rising temperature, she took off her nylon jacket with all the pockets, and his whole body tightened.

Okay, not like one of the kids, Jack acknowledged. Those were bona fide adult female curves under that plain T-shirt in an expensive fabric blend. But she was no less off-limits than one of the munchkins.

Yeah, she was a blonde, and he dug blondes. Her legs, in tailored khaki, tempted a man to imagine them naked or wrapped around his waist or resting on his shoulders.

But Jack knew his limitations. He didn't "do" good girls. He didn't go after the chardonnay and postgraduate degree type. And if he'd ever had any fantasies about making it with a princess, they hadn't gone beyond tenth grade, when he'd wrestled off Valerie Hardison's bra after the Boone High School production of *Once Upon a Mattress*.

Christina Sebastiani was a job. Maybe not even that, if he didn't like the look of the intelligence packet the old man put together.

Still, Jack could watch and admire and, in his own fashion, pay tribute.

He eased his camera from his pocket. It was a nice little Nikon, light and compact. Nothing like the sleek, inconspicuous numbers he'd carried on missions, with their high-speed film and low-light capabilities, but he'd left his toys, his cameras and guns, behind. Now he shot pictures with a thirty-five millimeter aperture and shot targets with a nine.

He played for a moment with framing and focus and then let his lens see for him. Whir and click on Christina, her profile sharp and perfect as a queen on a silver coin. Click on the slant of sunlight drifting through the trees. Whir and click to catch Eric, fingers cramped and tongue stuck out in concentration as he printed on a chart. Click on Christina again, her blond head bent forward as she conferred with two girls. Click on a willow, leaning down from the bank to trail pale leaves in the dark water. On Christina, laughing. Christina, stretching. Christina… glaring at him.

He lowered his camera.

She stalked toward him, her long legs making a statement of their own. "What are you doing?"

He couldn't figure what had tweaked her tail. But she was definitely upset. He answered honestly. "Taking pictures."

"Why?"

"Habit?" When she didn't smile, he shrugged and elaborated. "I used to be a photographer's mate. Only then it turned out the Teams needed a photography specialist, so I graduated to intelligence ops."

Her eyes widened. "You were spying on me?"

"Princess, if I were spying on you, you wouldn't catch me at it. I was taking pictures, that's all."

"What kind of pictures?"

"Trees. Water. Kids. What difference does it make?"

Her gaze slid sideways toward Eric, hunched over the clipboard a few yards away. His right ankle was stretched in front of him, propped on Jack's jacket and draped with a cold, wet sock.

"I'm sorry," she said stiffly. "I don't like having my picture taken."

So, maybe now was a bad time to confess that he had more than one shot of her. "Yeah, I could have guessed that," Jack drawled.

She blushed. He didn't know many women who still did that. He would have bet princesses didn't. "How is he?" she asked.

Jack tore his attention from the pretty pink color in her cheeks. Who? Oh, yeah. The kid. Eric.

"Not bad," Jack said. "Hard to tell how much damage was done until the swelling goes down. It hurts, and his toes are getting cold, but that'll teach him not to mess around near water."

"Will he be able to walk back to the bus?"

"Comfortably? Probably not. We'll see how he does once we get some ice on that ankle."

She nodded absently, her smooth, blond brows drawing together.

"Hey, it's okay," Jack said. "It was an accident. Could have happened on anybody's watch."

"I know that. It's just the children are my responsibility, and I feel…"

"Guilty?"

She frowned. "Concerned."

Jack leaned against the tree trunk at his back, satisfied he'd provoked her into forgetting all about his camera and her worries. "I didn't want you to fret about what I was thinking, that's all."

She looked at him like he was something scraped off the bottom of her royal shoe. "I am completely indifferent to what you think."

He grinned. "You don't look indifferent. You look—" he paused, enjoying her frost "—annoyed."

Another woman would have blown up at him. But Princess Cupcake held it together, held it in. Training, he thought. Not his kind of training, but he could still respect her discipline.

"Not at all. I appreciate your help with Eric." Her smile glinted, cool as water over rock. "And if he can't walk, I'll appreciate it even more."

An hour later, it was time for the kids to return to the bus for lunch and the ride back to school. And Eric couldn't walk.

Shouldn't walk, Jack told Christina. The pain was his body's way of warning him against putting weight on that ankle.

"All right." She didn't argue. He liked that about her, too. "Can you get him to the parking lot?"

Jack wanted to tell her it would be a piece of cake. He used to run holding a one-hundred-seventy-pound rubber boat over his head. He used to do sit-ups cradling a two-hundred-pound section of telephone pole. But then he'd been able to rely on his swim team. Then he'd been able to rely on his shoulder.

He looked at the white-faced Eric. One hundred thirty pounds, tops. "I can try."

"What can I do to help?"

"Stay out of our way."

Jack dumped ice by the side of the stream and retrieved his jacket from the ground. The kid couldn't hobble half a mile, even with support. A piggyback ride was out of the question. The docs who had stitched Jack together had carved a nice chunk from his back to replace the missing muscle in his left shoulder. But if he took the kid in a fireman's hold, he wouldn't need to rotate the shoulder. He could distribute the weight over his back and hips.

He lowered himself to one knee. "You've got to put your arms around my neck."

Standing behind him, Eric hesitated. "Maybe I could walk."

"Don't be a hero, kid. You'll regret it in the morning."

He heard his own tone, harsher than he intended, and saw Christina's eyes narrow. *Watch it, Flash.* Christina was sharp. Too sharp. He didn't want her guessing what was wrong with him. He didn't like her knowing there was anything wrong.

"Tell you what, next time you can carry me," he suggested lightly.

He was rewarded when Christina relaxed and Eric leaned against his back. Jack gripped the boy's arms against his chest and pushed to his feet.

And the first part of the trail was easy. He'd been working out, hadn't he? Lifting weights, just like the physical therapist had told him. Developing his damn range of motion. His legs were strong. And he was pumped to be in action again.

After they passed the quarter-mile mark, though, he could hear Eric puffing in discomfort. The hold put pressure on the boy's chest. It had to be pulling on his arms, too. He hung, a dead weight on Jack's back, his left foot occasionally bumping Jack's legs. Jack felt the stretch reach deep into his shoulder as scar tissue gave. Despite the cool temperature under the trees, he tasted sweat on his upper lip and felt it at the base of his spine.

Don't quit. Don't be a quitter. The words had kept him going during weeks of training on the beach at Coronado, during months of physical therapy in a well-lit room that stank of antiseptic and pain. And they'd worked then, because then he had believed that if he didn't quit he could be everything he wanted to be. He could be a SEAL.

He knew better now. He wasn't working for anything now. But he still didn't quit.

"Can we stop a minute?" Eric huffed in his ear.

Jack unclenched his jaw. "Sure, kid. Let me get to that log up there..." Fifteen steps, he thought. He could do another fifteen steps. No problem. "...and we'll take a break."

It was twenty-two steps, and when Jack lowered the big eighth grader onto the fallen tree, pain knifed from his shoulder to his hand. "Referred pain," the therapist called it. Jack had another word, but he couldn't use it in front of the kid.

He glanced down at the boy. Eric's face was really red. His mouth worked as he struggled not to cry.

Reluctant sympathy moved in Jack. "Breathe in through your nose," he instructed.

The kid, near tears and embarrassed, kept his head down, focusing on his wet, bare ankle.

"Come on," Jack urged. "In through your nose for a count of four, hold it for seven, breathe out for eight." He demonstrated. "Helps with the pain," he explained.

"How would you know?" the boy muttered. His eyes were wet.

"It worked when I was shot."

Eric looked up, diverted from his sulks and his swollen ankle. "Really?"

"Yeah. Try it. In, two, three, four. Hold...and out slow, six, seven, eight. Good. Again."

They matched breaths a couple more times, until the kid's shoulders relaxed and his unhealthy color faded.

"That's it," Jack encouraged. "Never let 'em see you sweat."

The boy swiped at his eyes with the back of his hand. "You're sweating."

"Yeah, well, that'll be our secret, okay?"

Eric gave him a shaky smile. "Okay."

"Is everything all right?"

Princess Cupcake had backtracked along the straggling line of students. Intent on the boy, Jack had not heard her approach. God, he really was slipping.

Concern warmed her big blue eyes. Jack stiffened. He didn't want her pity.

And he wasn't sacrificing the kid to her compassion, either. He remembered too well what it was to be thirteen and afraid that your voice or behavior would let you down, to have a man-size ego and feet, and a child's need to please.

"I needed a breather," he said. "So we stopped."

She studied them both, still with that gooey look in her eyes. How much had she heard?

"Is he too heavy for you?" she asked.

Jack would not be offended. She was being responsible, and he was—well, okay, he was a little offended. No SEAL had ever left behind a dead or wounded comrade. "What, are you going to carry him? He outweighs you by twenty pounds." He shook his head. "We're doing fine."

"We could make a chair of our arms and carry him that way."

It wasn't a bad idea. She probably could have gotten Eric out like that, changing bearers, if Jack hadn't happened along. But they were almost at the bus now. And a forearm carry would put a hell of a lot more stress on his shoulder than the fireman's hold.

"I told you, we're fine. I don't need your help."

She raised her eyebrows. "Very well. I certainly

wouldn't want to interfere with you flexing your very impressive set of muscles. I'll meet you in the parking lot.''

She swept up his jacket and stalked down the trail, leaving him behind to admire her classy comeback and her heart-shaped rear end.

Chapter 3

The man was impossible.

And nearly impossible to get rid of.

Christina marched into the office she shared with three other postgraduate fellows and snatched her mail from her cubbyhole.

Jack Dalton strolled through the door behind her, exuding pheromones and disapproval. "You should lock your door."

She would not let him see how he rattled her. "Would it do any good?" she asked sweetly.

He grinned, that sharp, attractive grin that hooked her insides. "Trying to get rid of me, princess?"

She barricaded herself behind her battered metal desk. "Not very effectively, obviously. I haven't had this much difficulty shaking my bodyguard since I was thirteen years old and had to climb the garden wall."

He stuck his hands in his pockets, taking a slow survey

of the shabby room. "What were you running away from that time?"

What harm could it do to tell him? "A British film crew. They were making a documentary about my mother."

"Did you get caught?"

She lifted her chin. "Not until they finished filming for the day."

He eyed her appraisingly. "That must have gone over big with your parents."

"My mother was very understanding. Besides, the crew got what they came for. My parents were gracious, my brother was dashing, Anna looked adorable and Julia impressed the interviewer with her grasp of public affairs."

"The perfect family."

"The perfect royal family. Yes."

"And where do you fit in?"

She almost said, "I don't." She shrugged instead. "Is it necessary to fit in?"

"For most kids, yeah. Julia... That's your older sister, right?"

"Two years older and wiser and prettier."

"Jealous?"

"No. Not really. When I was thirteen, perhaps. Julia had so much more poise. And breasts," she added, surprising both of them with her honesty. "Julia had breasts."

He laughed, sharp and quick, and heat surged to her face. What had she been thinking, to blurt that out?

"You've got breasts," he drawled.

She looked down at the mail on her lap. "I didn't then. What I had was baby fat."

"I bet you were cute."

She shook her head. "Thirteen-year-old girls do not want to be cute."

"What do they want?"

She didn't want to remember. She was beyond that now. She was a respected member of the academic community, with a purpose and identity that reached far beyond the confining walls of the palace. The awkward, pudgy princess had morphed into cool, assured *Dr.* Sebastiani. And she did not discuss old dreams, old hurts and her breasts with her father's hired keeper.

"This is an inappropriate discussion," she said stiffly.

"Why? What did you want, princess, when you were thirteen?"

She straightened her shoulders and told him part of the truth. "To be left alone."

He hooked a chair from behind an empty desk and straddled it, his blue gaze steady on her face. "So, some things don't change."

"No," she agreed, and ignored the pang at her heart. "Some things never change."

"Where do we go from here?"

"We don't." She began to sort her mail, stacking the first-class envelopes on her desk, setting aside the department memos to be dealt with later. "There is no 'we.' I expect you to report back to my father that you found me well and safe and happy, and that your services are not required."

"I don't report to your father. I report to mine. And until I hear from him, I don't know what's required."

Christina fidgeted with the neat stack of envelopes. There was one from the Harborside Hotel in San Diego, which she hoped held her conference confirmation, and a plain white envelope with no return address. Responding to either seemed preferable to dealing with Jack Dalton right now.

She tore open the white envelope and unfolded the single sheet inside. A newspaper clipping fell into her lap. She scanned the headline, her heart thumping unpleasantly.

And all her brave assertions turned bitter in her mouth.

Something was wrong.

Jack felt it in his gut.

And yet Christina hadn't moved, hadn't said a word. She breathed slowly, in and out, and her spine and her eyes were straight. But there was tension in her shoulders, and her gaze did not focus on the paper she held. The edges trembled in her tightened grip.

Inside him, something lurched in acknowledgment, both of her distress and her determination to hide it. But Christina had already made it clear she didn't want his sympathy. Or his admiration. Or anything to do with him.

"Somebody die?" he asked.

She stiffened. "I don't know what you're talking about."

He gestured toward the letter she still held. "Something's upset you."

She gave him one of those "Me, princess. You, peasant" looks she was so good at. "You've been upsetting me since you got here."

He almost grinned. "Something else."

"It's nothing." She grimaced slightly. "Fan mail."

He held out his hand. "Let me see."

When she didn't respond, he leaned forward and tugged the paper away.

U.S. Embassy Bombed, the headline read.

It was an undated Associated Press wire clipping from Montebello. Jack read it carefully, comparing what the reporter knew with what his father had told him. *No group has claimed responsibility for the bombing, although sev-*

*eral terrorist organizations in the region are known to be
hostile to the U.S. military presence in Montebello...*

Right. Jack's dad had said Sheik Ahmed Kamal of
Tamir was the most likely suspect. King Marcus was convinced of the neighboring ruler's guilt. And Kamal was
well known for his anti-West sentiment.

Jack read on. *A source close to the palace reveals that
the bombing could have been a diversion to cover a kidnap
attempt on Princess Julia.*

Oh, boy. A leak at the palace must have made the old
man unhappy, Jack thought. But he was going to be really
ticked about the straggling line of cut-out letters pasted
below the article, like a ransom note in a B movie: THIS
COULD BE YOU.

Hell.

"We've got to get this tested," he said.

Christina raised her eyebrows. She had her emotions in
check again. He couldn't help wondering what it would
take to shatter that calm control. "Tested for what?"

"For fingerprints. ID. To find out who's threatening
you."

She sighed. "No one's threatened me."

Exasperation spiked his voice. "What do you call this?"

"An unfortunate consequence of my family's fame. I
get them all the time, Mr. Dalton, even here. Requests for
autographs, marriage proposals, nude videos, pleas for
money... I refuse to get rattled by one more crank who
likes to cut things out of the newspaper."

But she had been rattled. He'd seen it in her eyes.

"You better start calling me Jack," he said. "I have a
feeling we're going to get to know each other pretty well."

"No. I told you, I don't need a bodyguard."

"And I don't need a princess with attitude. But it looks
like neither one of us is going to get what we want. Will

you at least cooperate until we establish whether or not you're a target?''

She bit her lip. He couldn't tell if she was responding to his jibe or considering his offer. "How long would that take?''

"You want the truth?''

"Of course.''

"I don't know. I've got a report from the major hitting my post office box, maybe today. Background stuff. Probably an update on the bombing investigation. I can go over that and tell you what kind of risk I think you're taking. And then we get lab results on your little love letter here. If we establish a tie to Kamal, I'd say you're in real danger. After that, it's up to you whether you accept help or not.''

"*Your* help.''

He shrugged, trying not to care that he was being judged and found wanting. Trying not to care whether he saved her pretty neck or not. He was out of the save-the-world business. "Doesn't have to be me. Get yourself a nice professional with a suit and a shoulder holster, if you want. Maybe a woman. I'm just passing through.''

"On your way to where?''

Nowhere, he thought.

"Does it matter?'' he asked bleakly. His shoulder ached, a promise of pain tomorrow. "All you need to know is whether I'm available and if I'm qualified.''

She tipped her head to one side, showing off the long, elegant line of her throat. "I believe we determined your qualifications yesterday. And you have made yourself annoyingly available.''

He grimaced, thinking of what that availability had cost him. Damn near everything. "Oh, I'm available, all right.''

She nodded. "Very well, then.''

"Very well, what?''

"I accept your protection until my danger is disproved." His surprise must have registered, because a small, remote smile touched the corners of her mouth. "I'm not stupid, Mr. Dalton…Jack. Just stubborn. I don't want to get kidnapped, and I don't intend to be used as a bargaining chip in whatever feud Sheik Ahmed has with my father."

"So, you'll…cooperate?"

"Yes. With the understanding that you will not interfere with my work."

He looked at the neat stacks of paper on her desk, the sharpened pencils and a hunk of glittering rock. "What kind of work do you do? You're a microbiologist, right?"

A brief gleam appeared in her blue eyes. Amused, but not malicious. "Microbial ecologist. My research focuses on isolating and identifying microorganisms—bacteria—in the soil that could help plants thrive in metal-contaminated areas."

"Yeah, I can see how you couldn't let that slide for a few days," he drawled.

"Actually, microorganisms are crucial to ecosystem function. An understanding of their role in plant success could have huge implications in developing land-reclamation strategies."

Her enthusiasm was kind of cute. He wasn't going to argue with her. Hell, he wasn't even sure he understood her.

"Fine. You do that. After we go to the post office. I want to pick up the report from the major so I can read up on the situation. And we need to send this letter in for prints."

"Send it where?"

"To my old man. Might as well use the connections we've got. Do you have plastic bags in that lab of yours?"

She nodded. "I use sterile bags to collect soil samples."

"Great. We'll bag this and the envelope it came in. I'll need to send our prints, too, so they can eliminate them."

Her eyes widened. "You carry fingerprint equipment?"

"No, but any unglazed paper will hold prints, and they can lift them with ninhydrin."

"How do you know that?"

"You have your area of expertise, I've got mine. You pick up a lot on counterterrorist ops."

"I'm sure you do," she said dryly. "Excuse me if I don't have your experience."

He couldn't resist. It was a knee-jerk reaction to the challenge of her, the precision of her speech and the delicacy of her scent and the angle of her chin.

"Princess, anytime you want experience, I'm your man."

Jack pushed open the door to his motel room. The trapped air rushed to greet them, smelling like mildew and pine cleaner and sex by the hour.

Christina recoiled.

He looked over his shoulder impatiently. "Problem?"

Her nerves jangled. She took a deep breath and a step forward. *Chin up.* "Not really. I'm just not in the habit of accompanying strange men to their motel rooms."

He grinned and tossed the package from Uncle Jonathan onto the cheap dresser. "Well, that's a relief."

She lifted her eyebrows in question.

"As long as I'm responsible for your safety, it's good to know you don't indulge in high-risk behavior."

She couldn't think of anything riskier than this close association with Captain Experience. Except maybe getting herself kidnapped by Ahmed Kamal.

Jack Dalton was too much. Too big, too blunt, too muscled and far too sure of himself. He made her feel like a trembling virgin. The feeling wasn't helped at all by the depressing knowledge that she was a virgin and far too close to trembling....

"I'll leave the risk taking to you." She looked around for someplace to sit. There were clothes folded on the room's only chair. She felt it would be presumptuous to move them, to handle his pants and his socks. Primly, she sat on the very edge of his bed. "From now on, you can catch all the bullets and infectious diseases."

"You've got the wrong idea about my lifestyle, princess."

"It's possible." She crossed her legs, enjoying a faint, unfamiliar thrill when his eyes followed the movement. "It's also possible you have the wrong idea about mine."

"Maybe we both have something to learn."

His rough voice snagged all her nerve endings. Maybe. Maybe Jack Dalton could teach her all the wild, wonderful, wicked things other women learned from men.

And maybe she should take a rock and knock some sense into her head first. It would be equally painful and ultimately less destructive.

"Not from each other. This situation is difficult enough without our playing at some ill-judged sexual attraction."

He shoved his hands into his pockets. "Ill-judged, huh?"

"Extremely ill-judged," she answered firmly.

"Yeah, I guess you're right. But, princess—" he waited until she dragged her gaze up to his "—if and when I do make a move, I won't be playing."

He disappeared into the bathroom. "I'm going to pack my kit," he called. "Make yourself at home."

Well.

Christina sat on the shiny motel spread, her knees crossed, and wondered if she should be flattered by his near pass or run screaming from the room. Neither, she decided. Dalton was probably just trying to sweet-talk her into going along with whatever he wanted. And if Sheik Ahmed were after her, running away was the worst thing she could do.

She needed facts. A scientist did not draw conclusions before compiling all her data. She needed information to assess her own danger. And the information she needed was sitting in an overnight mail envelope on the dresser three feet away.

She uncrossed her legs and stood. She picked the packet off the maple laminate and weighed it in her hand. Jonathan Dalton's name was on the return label, along with an address in Texas. She turned the envelope over. Tape sealed the flap. She was testing it with her fingernail when she got that feeling again, the warm sensation of being watched.

She looked up.

Jack stood in the bathroom doorway, one shoulder propped against the jamb. His face was expressionless. His eyes were annoyed. "Was that addressed to you?"

Heat swept up her cheeks. She lifted her chin.

"If it's about me," she said, "then it's my business."

He prowled forward and tugged the envelope from her grasp. "Wrong. You told me you didn't want me interfering with your work. Well, don't interfere with mine."

"I have a right to know what your father has found out. I should know if the situation warrants my taking precautions."

"You don't have the experience to judge that. I do. But if there's anything in there you need to see, I'll show it to you."

It was more than she expected. Better, perhaps, than she deserved. She sat again, cautiously, on the bed.

Jack sat beside her. She tried not to notice how his jeans pulled across his thighs, how the mattress sank under his weight and rolled her toward him. Ridiculous. She was twenty-seven years old, and she'd never sat with a man on his bed before. She inched away.

"Uncomfortable?" he murmured.

"No," she lied.

"Because we can wait till we get back to your place to do this."

"I can't." She laughed shakily at herself, at the whole situation. "I couldn't even wait for you to get your things together. Besides, if we find out you're mistaken—if there is no real danger—then there's no need for you to come to my place."

"Right, then." He ripped the envelope open.

She saw a dark blue portfolio with her name on the cover and an eight-by-ten glossy of the formal portrait commemorating her twenty-first birthday. The girl in the photo wore a long white gown and a glittering tiara and what Christina thought of as her "public" face: eyes straight, chin up, mouth bent in a smile.

Jack studied it. "You tick off the royal photographer, princess?"

She was surprised. "No."

"Because a portrait is supposed to engage the viewer with the subject. This shot is dead. You look like you're posing for the five-dollar bill." He turned the glossy over. "No wonder you don't like having your picture taken."

He didn't know the half of it, she thought ruefully. He had no idea how hard she worked on that invulnerable, plastic, public pose. She didn't want him to know.

"I've got your bio here," he said. "You don't need to see that. Transcripts—UCLA, Montana, very impressive—

physical description, distinguishing marks…'' He grinned suddenly. ''No tattoos?''

Reluctantly, she smiled back. ''No. But I have a scar on the inside of my elbow from playing Saracens and Crusaders with my brother.'' She twisted her arm for him to see. Concentrating on an old hurt to conceal the fresh pain of her brother's disappearance.

''Nice,'' Jack said. ''When we get to know each other better, I'll show you mine.''

She wondered where under his clothes he carried his scars. And blushed again. She cleared her throat. ''You were wounded?''

''Yeah.'' He riffled through more papers.

''Recently?''

''Four months ago.''

''Where?'' she asked, and then held her breath at the inappropriateness of her question.

But Jack didn't appear to notice. ''Philippines,'' he answered briefly as he continued to scan the contents of the envelope. ''Here we go.''

She breathed again. ''What?''

''An account of the bombing. This guy they caught in conjunction with the embassy bombing, this Muhammad Oman, is some kind of freelance terrorist.''

''And?''

''And when he was interrogated, he fingered Sheik Ahmed Kamal as his boss. Which means your father has good reason for his suspicions.'' He fell silent, eyes and fingers skimming the page.

''What are you reading now?''

''Background on the feud between Montebello and Tamir…real soap opera stuff, isn't it?''

She drew herself up. ''You can say that. But Sheik Ahmed's claim to our land raises issues of natural resources and regional stability. And your government in Washington agrees, or they would not be so anxious to keep the peace.''

''Plus there's the little matter of a U.S. military base on the southeastern end of the island,'' Jack drawled.

She didn't back down. ''Precisely.''

''Look, I'm not getting paid to worry about national security anymore. I'm supposed to worry about yours.''

''Unless there's a connection, you're wasting your time.''

He flipped over another page. ''Time's one thing I've...'' His voice failed.

''What? What is it?''

He was staring at the portfolio on his lap. The angle of the cover hid its contents from her, but she saw a corner of newsprint and knew, suddenly, sickeningly, what he had found.

The other picture taken the year she turned twenty-one.

She couldn't see the headline. It didn't matter. The same enlarged, grainy image had appeared on the front cover of every tabloid and on the inside pages of every entertainment rag in the world. Six years later, it still had the power to freeze her stomach and make a man look at her with hot speculation in his eyes.

Jack didn't look at her at all, and that was almost worse. ''More background,'' he said tersely, and closed the folder.

Damn, she was beautiful.

Even when she was swathed in a white lab coat, with her hair pulled back and plastic goggles around her neck, Christina had what it took to make Jack sweat.

But the image he'd just seen—Christina topless, emerging from a lake at dawn, with every fantasy-inspired curve gilded by the sun—was enough to make him drool.

To make him ache.

To make him beg.

The shot must have been snapped with a zoom from a distance and then blown up to meet tabloid requirements. But picture quality wouldn't have been the first thing on the photographer's mind, or the mind of any man who saw the final product. Christina stood knee-deep in the dark water, proud head lifted, legs apart. She looked like a pagan goddess rising from the lake to claim a human lover. Her full, proud breasts glistened. Her wet hair poured down her back like sunshine. Her wet bikini bottoms clung to her like skin. And the water was obviously cold.

Jack's tongue felt too big for his mouth. His jeans felt too tight.

Christina was saying something. Asking him something. "What is it?"

"More background." He closed the folder before he embarrassed himself.

Confronting Christina's sheer physical perfection made him sharply aware of how much he had lost. The sniper in the Philippines had blown away more than his shoulder and his career. The terrorist bastard had hacked at his confidence.

He could still walk away, he thought. He was just passing through.

"Let's go to your apartment," he said. "I need to call my old man."

Chapter 4

It figured that the exiled princess of Montebello didn't live in an apartment. Jack realized his mistake as soon as Christina swung her new-model pickup truck onto a private road flanked by stone columns. A discreet plaque identified the entrance to Eagle's Nest Residential Community. *No Soliciting,* the sign said. Not *Welcome.*

The truck swooped down curves and up hills. Through stands of tall, dark trees, wide windows flashed. Jack glimpsed piles of rock and spires of wood, some natural, some man-made.

They sure didn't look like any graduate student digs he'd ever seen.

He was way out of his league here, he thought grimly. What had Christina called it? *Some ill-judged sexual attraction.* Yeah.

And yet every time he looked at her—hell, even when he didn't—he got this brain-fog image of her rising out of the lake, her magnificent body covered with water and sunshine and not much else. She had great breasts. He looked across at her aristocratic profile and imagined her wearing one skimpy nylon triangle. He looked out at the scenery and imagined her naked.

And the pictures in his head were making him cross-eyed.

He rubbed the back of his neck, where the muscles cramped as his shoulder stiffened. Focus, he ordered himself. Before he'd left the SEALs, his survival and the survival of his team had depended on his ability to concentrate. Now...well, hers might.

That realization cleared his brain, at least temporarily. He sat up as Christina maneuvered into a sunken driveway and shifted the truck into Park. Her garage was buried in the side of a hill. A stone walk wound from the drive to the house, all angles and cedar and glass.

Whoa. Jack climbed out. Looked up. "Nice place you've got here."

Christina's face got that frosty look he was beginning to realize covered self-consciousness. "The house was one of my father's conditions for my remaining at the university. It has a state-of-the-art security system."

He bet it did. Not that that would stop a terrorist. Not that it could stop him or Merlin or Crack or any of the SEALs, if they had time and the inclination to break in. Jack followed her up a hill landscaped with ferns and wild-flowers. She had a nice...walk. The soaring windows overhead reflected back the red and gold of the afternoon sun.

Once upon a time there was a princess who lived in a tower....

She unlocked the massive door. The foyer was flagstone, paneled in some light wood and pierced with windows. She pressed a security code into the keypad by the door.

"No armed guards at the gate?" Jack asked dryly.

Her eyes gleamed with humor. He liked that, liked that she was able to laugh at herself. "The only communities in Montana with armed guards are survivalist compounds. Even my father drew the line at my living in one of those. Please." She stepped forward briskly, like a White House tour guide. "Make yourself at home."

He grimaced. "Right."

Home had never looked like this.

It wasn't that the Daltons didn't have money. Jonathan Dalton may have been a lousy husband and father, but he was a great provider. His wife, Clara, had filled her empty days with shopping, her empty home with velvet sofas and walnut tables and china doodads.

Jack parked his seabag at the bottom of the curving staircase and pivoted slowly, taking in Christina's wide-open living room: cordovan leather couches and deco lamps, bleached wood floors and rich carpets. Paintings hung like jewels on the high white walls. He didn't know a whole lot about art, but that one over the fireplace, all curving blues and greens, looked like a Chagall. And he'd bet the ranch it wasn't a copy.

Oh, yeah. Out of his league and in over his head. He stuck his hands in his pockets.

"I'm sorry if it's not…" Christina hesitated. "I don't have time to spend on housekeeping. And my cleaning service won't be in until Monday."

She wasn't serious. Was she? What did she think—that he was going to order her to stand inspection?

"I left the white gloves behind with the uniform, princess. But if you're looking for compliments, you've got a really nice place here. Classy. You want me to take off my shoes?"

She tipped her chin up. "Of course not. I…the phone's

in the kitchen,'' she said, and escaped across the Oriental carpet.

The red sun bled through the tall windows on either side of the fireplace. Jack glanced out on a tumble of rocks and plants. Plenty of cover for a sniper there. He wondered if her glass was bulletproof.

"Can I get you something to drink?" she asked.

"Yeah. Thanks."

"Whiskey? Wine? Tea?"

He cradled the receiver between his neck and shoulder, fishing in his wallet for his father's number. "Got any beer?"

"I'm sorry. No."

For a princess, she sure was quick to apologize. He shook his head. "Never mind. Water is fine."

He listened to the phone ring on the other end of the line.

And ring. Jonathan Dalton wasn't home. Well, that figured. For sixteen years, the old man had never been around when Jack wanted him. Of course, a couple of months after Jack's mother died, the major had decided to take a stab at fatherhood, and that had been even worse.

Jack depressed the phone hook and dialed again, aware of Christina pulling glasses from the cupboard behind him.

"Global Enterprises," the receptionist chirped. "How may I direct your call?"

"Jonathan Dalton, please."

"May I tell him who's calling?"

"Jack Dalton."

"Who?"

He heard his teeth snap together. "His son."

Christina put his water on the counter by his hand. Her warm fingers left imprints on the cold glass. He nodded thanks and picked it up as a different female voice came on the line.

"Mr. Dalton? This is Elizabeth Landry, your father's executive assistant. He's not available to take your call right now. May I help you?"

Jack put the water down untasted. "No. Thanks. Tell him he can reach me at this number, please." He rattled off the number on Christina's phone. "Got that? Yeah. Anytime tonight. Thanks." He hung up the phone and found Christina watching him, her mermaid hair and wide blue eyes like something out of a sailor's fantasy.

His fantasies. Smooth, dark water around long, pale thighs...

Don't go there, Flash.

"I can't reach the old man. Looks like we'll have to wait for him to call us."

"Do you know when he'll be back?"

"No." He couldn't decipher the faint question in her eyes. Surprise? Disapproval? "We're not exactly close," he said.

"Why is that?"

He didn't want to go into it. Not ever, and especially not with Princess Perfect here. But given that he'd just been drooling over the illustrated story of her life, it seemed only fair to give her a quick and dirty rundown on The Daltons: the Dysfunctional Years.

"When my father decided he'd finally had enough of selling his services to the highest bidder, I was sixteen years old and full of myself. I was used to being the man of the house. Nobody was going to tell me what to do, especially not some guy I didn't set eyes on more than once a year. We had a couple of years with him playing the heavy father and me acting like the jerk son before he decided to ship me off to West Point and let the army turn me into an officer and a gentleman.''

She regarded him steadily. Her interest warmed him, made him awkward. ''And was your army up for this enormous task?''

He shrugged. ''We'll never know. I ran off and enlisted in the navy.''

''Your father—he was upset?''

''He was a hypocrite. He was enlisted. Went mustang in Korea.''

Her blond brows drew together. ''What does that mean? 'Mustang'?''

''It's a term for an enlisted man who comes up through the ranks and makes the jump to officer. It doesn't happen often.''

''And because he did it, you wanted to do the same. You wanted to make him proud of you.''

Jack shrugged uncomfortably. ''It wasn't that. I just didn't want him using his money, his influence, to get me an officer's berth. I didn't want what he could do for me.''

Christina smiled ruefully. ''Yes. I understand. Still, to give up your chance for a college education...''

''When I was eighteen, my head so stuffed with big ideas, a college education would have been wasted on me.''

''Learning is never wasted,'' she said firmly.

She would think that. She was a microbiologist. Microbial ecologist, he corrected himself. She probably had enough letters after her name to qualify as a government program.

''I went back for it six years later,'' he said, surprising them both by his need to explain. ''Night school. I had the discipline for it then.''

''You got your degree while you were a SEAL?''

The disbelief in her voice made him wince. He should have kept his trap shut. "It's not that unusual. When you're a SEAL, you've got to be the best."

"You make me a little ashamed," she said softly. "I never had to combine classes with work. All I've ever done is study."

"Well, you must be good at it. Made good grades. Got a good job."

"Yes." She gave him a small, twisted smile that sneaked inside him. "I'm a much better scientist than I am a princess."

Oh, no. He was not going to fall for that poor-little-princess routine. He was not going to fall for her. "What kind of cook are you?"

The smile froze. "I beg your pardon?"

"Dinner. We're stuck here till the phone rings, and we have to eat. Do you cook?"

Christina blinked, bewildered by his abrupt change of subject. One minute she'd been having a real conversation, basking in the uncommon intimacy of actually talking with a man in her kitchen, and now he expected her to feed him? She reached for her dignity.

"Not well. I can offer you some eggs and toast if you're hungry."

"I'm more hungry than eggs and toast. Do you mind if I see what else you've got?"

She stepped back, waving a hand in a gesture she hoped would look royal, and probably came off as royally ticked. "Please. Be my guest. But don't expect to find anything. I told you, I'm no cook."

He was already rummaging through cupboards without regard to her privacy or her warning. She stifled a protest.

He flashed a grin over his shoulder. "Yeah, but I am."

She was still trying to take it in. "You cook."

"You bet."

"That's very...evolved of you."

"Not really. Cooking is just another way to be self-sufficient. I did a lot of the cooking growing up."

Trying not to resent his intrusion, she watched him pile things on her counter, her clean, bare counter, like testaments to her sad, bare life: an unopened box of macaroni and cheese, a flat tin of anchovies she used to spice up pizza, two cans of tuna and a small bottle of cocktail olives with a Montebello label. He dug deeper, unearthing her lonely bottle of olive oil and the dried herbs she'd bought to make salad dressing.

"Your mother didn't cook?" she asked.

"My mom liked to go out. She was the uncrowned benefit queen and committee chair of Highland Park, Texas." He squatted to dig in a cupboard for a stainless steel pot. "My sister and I got pretty tired of heating things in the microwave, so I taught myself the basics."

After filling the pot at the sink, he set it on the stove. Christina sipped her water, watching him. He poured olive oil into a skillet and peeled garlic with a no-fuss ease that was impressive. His T-shirt stretched over his biceps. His forearms were muscled. She found herself watching them, and the movement of his hands, and flushed.

"That doesn't look very basic," she said.

"I had an XO—executive officer—who liked to cook. I learned a lot from him."

He scraped slivered garlic into the hot oil. The scent rose and made her mouth water.

"It always seemed a waste of time for me to cook," she said. "It's not like I was ever going to be called on to whip up a formal state dinner, and here...most of the time, I eat alone."

He chopped anchovies with brisk competence. "All the

more reason to make sure you eat properly, then. Weren't you the woman who said learning is never wasted?''

"I guess I did," she admitted. Whatever he was making smelled too good for her to take offense. But she'd never taken kindly to being told what to do, and she couldn't resist teasing him a little. "But in this case it would still be superfluous. I have you to take care of me now. At least temporarily."

He slid her a dark, unreadable look. "I didn't sign on as your houseboy, princess."

"No." She was embarrassed. And it served her right, for trying to flirt with a man like Jack Dalton. "I didn't mean—I don't expect you to wait on me."

"Why not?"

"Well, I—I very much doubt my father wants to hire you because you're a good cook or can run errands. I may need a bodyguard, but I can live without servants. I *prefer* to live without servants."

"So you moved to Montana to get away from it all."

She hesitated. "Something like that."

He added salt to the boiling water and then threw in the uncooked noodles from the box of macaroni and cheese. "You said you had wine. White?"

Here, at least, she could demonstrate her expertise. "I have a bottle of 1997 Laspiro Classico."

"Is that good?"

"The best. It's a Montebellan wine."

He dumped the tuna in the simmering skillet and stirred. "You know, I haven't figured you out yet."

She stiffened. "Figured me out?"

"Yeah. You've got all these contradictions. You move nine thousand miles away from home, but you're obviously proud of the place. You take a job that shuts you up alone in a lab all day, but you're great with kids. You're pinup gorgeous, but you don't like having your picture taken. It makes a guy wonder where you're coming from."

She would not be threatened by his casual dissection. She handed him the wine bottle, saying, as lightly as she could, "I hate to disappoint you, but you haven't been hired to protect some international woman of mystery. I'm a very ordinary research scientist."

He lifted one of those wicked, dark eyebrows. "Ordinary?"

"Ordinary," she repeated firmly.

He added wine to the sauce. "I don't think so. Maybe you'd like to be ordinary. But I think you're more complicated than that."

Her heart beat faster. "Thank you for your amateur analysis, but I'm really indifferent to your opinion."

He shook his head. "You're not acting indifferent. You're acting defensive."

"Rubbish."

He grinned at her. "See?"

She managed to hold back her smile. The man did not need her encouragement. "Are you finished?"

"Almost. The pasta needs another five minutes," he said, deliberately misunderstanding her.

And in no more time than that, they were sitting down to the dinner he'd prepared, tuna in a savory wine-and-anchovy sauce over shell noodles.

"This is wonderful," Christina said honestly after the first mouthful. "I can't believe you just made it up with what was in my pantry."

"I used an old SEAL recipe for mission success—analyze, prioritize, improvise," Jack said.

Misgiving shook her. It sounded like something her policy-wise father would say. She didn't want to live her life according to someone else's formula. She put down her fork. "And which are we doing now?"

"Right now, we're eating dinner," he answered calmly. "But if you're talking about your situation, we're still analyzing. We improvise after I get an update from the old man."

As if on cue, the telephone rang.

Jack felt a familiar adrenaline rush. In one quick, smooth move, he was around the table and reaching for the wall phone. Christina was nearer, but he was faster. His hand covered hers on the receiver.

They were close, close enough for him to track the color creeping into her cheeks, but she held her ground and his gaze. "I'm still capable of answering my own phone, Mr. Dalton. Jack."

Hell, he knew that. But he wanted to protect her from whatever was out there, whoever was on the other end of the line.

Not his job anymore.

Not his fight anymore.

He would make his report and... What? Turn the assignment over to somebody else? The thought left a sour taste in his mouth.

He shrugged and released her. "Whatever you say, princess."

"Hello? Uncle Jonathan." Christina's voice was warm and gracious. "How are you? Where are you?"

He studied the contradictions of her face as she talked: her soft mouth and stubborn chin, her curved cheek and straight brows, the unexpected intelligence in those wide, Barbie doll eyes. Complicated, he'd called her, and he'd always chosen simple women and basic sex.

But he found he could not walk away.

"Yes, he's here," she was saying. "Yes, I understand,

but— All right, I'll listen. You take care, too." She held out the phone to Jack. "He wants to talk to you now."

He took the receiver. "Fill me in on what's going on."

"Jack." His father's voice, hearty and vigorous, flowed down the line. "How's the shoulder?"

It hurt like a son of a bitch, the muscle protesting, the scarred tissue stretched from carrying Eric Hunter half a mile to the bus.

By tomorrow, it would be a frozen block of pain. But Jack didn't bare his weaknesses to his father.

"Still attached. You get anything else out of this Oman guy?"

There was a pause. And then, with a sigh, his father accepted Jack's lead. "Muhammad Oman definitely planted the embassy bomb. There are at least eight terrorist groups active in the region, and he's got ties to four. He claims to have been hired by Ahmed Kamal this time."

"So, you go after Kamal."

"It's not that easy. Obviously, we're seeking diplomatic solutions. The United States is involved, but Kamal distrusts the West. And he still insists he's innocent."

As a former covert operative, Jack was deeply cynical about world leaders' claims of innocence, but he respected his father's judgment. "Could he be telling the truth?"

"We haven't been able to prove a link so far." Jonathan Dalton sounded weary. "And now Sheik Ahmed's demanding a meeting with King Marcus to discuss the future of his heir."

"What heir?"

"Princess Julia is pregnant with the sheik's grandchild."

Jack whistled. "All in the family, huh?"

"It's not funny, Jack," Jonathan said sharply. "Apparently Julia had a liaison with the sheik's son before he disappeared. She broke down and admitted it after the kidnap attempt. Marcus is furious.''

It was hard to care. Jack didn't know the king or Julia. The whole thing sounded like one of those glitzy soap operas that Janey used to watch in the evenings when their mother was out. Only this time the drama threatened Christina's safety. And Jack found he did care about that. A lot.

"So, when is this meeting between Marcus and Kamal?"

"Hard to say. The king refuses to negotiate until Sheik Ahmed will guarantee the safety of every single member of the royal family."

Jack shifted the receiver to his other ear to ease the strain on his shoulder. Christina stood two feet away, her blue eyes watchful, her full lips pressed together. His gut tightened. Deliberately, he looked away. "But if the sheik is innocent, he shouldn't mind promising that."

"He claims he can't. He says he has no responsibility for the attacks and no control over what happens in the future."

"That sounds almost like a threat."

"That's how the king is taking it."

"Christina got a threat today in the mail," Jack said abruptly. "I sent it to you for fingerprinting."

Jonathan Dalton expressed his opinion of that in one pungent sentence. For once, Jack thought, he and his father were in agreement. "Any identification?"

Christina was scowling at him. Jack turned his back on her. "A California postmark. I sent the envelope, too."

"How is she?" His father's concern sounded real. Personal. Completely out of character for Major Daddy Dalton.

Jack kept his voice cool. "Fine. She thinks the sender is a kook."

"What do you think?"

"I don't know. There was a pretty specific tie-in to the kidnap attempt. I'd say we have to treat the threat seriously until we find out who's behind it."

"All right." The major's rapid acceptance disconcerted Jack. His father had never demonstrated much respect for his opinions before. "Until we have guarantees from Kamal, we need to assume she's in danger. We'll work on identifying the letter. Marcus will want her to have round-the-clock protection."

"Fine. Hire someone."

"I thought I had."

"I just agreed to look into the situation for you."

"Don't you feel any personal responsibility at all?" his father demanded in a tone that went back to Jack's last year of high school, to bitter fights over broken curfews, traffic tickets and neglected homework. Jack felt a surge of instinctive, habitual resentment.

"Oh, that's rich, coming from you."

"We have a significant stake in this, Jack."

"Yeah? I thought you weren't playing mercenary anymore. How much did it take to pull you out of retirement?"

Jonathan's voice got colder than the sea before sunup. "That's not the issue. I have a personal obligation to the king."

"Along with a nice chunk of his kingdom."

"Marcus rewarded us all with tracts of land when he ascended to the throne. And may I point out that you will inherit that land one day?"

It all came down to money. It always came down to money. His heroic father had paid for his frequent absences from home with a bigger house, better schools, more pocket money.

"I don't want it," Jack said. "I don't want anything from you." *Except your time.* "You never got that."

"If you won't consider your own interests on the island, you might think about what further instability will do to our U.S. military presence there."

Great. If greed doesn't work, appeal to patriotism.

"You don't give up, do you?" Jack asked bitterly.

"Not when it comes to you, son."

The old hypocrite.

"You'll have to hire yourself another puppet, Dad. I'm out of the defense business, remember?" He pivoted to hang up.

And found Christina blocking his way. Damn.

What had she heard? What did she assume?

There was no expression on her pale, perfect face, but her eyes were sharp and bright. "It was up to me, you said."

He covered the mouthpiece of the receiver. "What?"

Her chin lifted a degree. "Back in my office. You said that once we determined that I was a target, it was up to me whether or not I accepted your help."

"I also said you could get yourself a professional bodyguard. A woman, maybe. Ex-Secret Service, somebody like that."

"Someone available and someone qualified, you said."

"Jack?" His father's voice rasped in his ear. "What the hell is going on?"

"Damned if I know. Hang on a minute." Jack shifted his hand on the receiver. "Are you saying you want me?"

She turned pink. "I want some control over how I'm going to spend my life for the next couple of days or weeks or months. At least I know you. And you won't keep me in a box."

"I'd like to," he muttered.

"But you haven't," she said.

"So, you want me because I'm ineffective, is that it?"

"You were quite effective today with Eric. I trust you to let me live my life while you take care of saving it." A smile crept into her eyes, into her voice, irresistible as a bar after a six-month tour at sea. "And you can cook," she said.

Chapter 5

There was no palace protocol for inviting a man to bed.

Not *her* bed, of course, Christina thought.

She had not lost all sense of decorum. She had not lost all sense of self-preservation. But as she led Jack up the stairs to the guest room, she wondered if she had lost her mind. Shuffled it into that stack of department memos building on her desk or dropped it down a mine shaft.

She'd acted impulsively, out of a need to control the situation and a misguided, misplaced compassion. Something in Jack's voice had plucked an answering chord inside her. *You'll have to hire yourself another puppet, Dad.*

And Christina, vibrating with empathy, hadn't stopped to consider what it would mean to have casual, confident, *über*-male Jack Dalton in her house. In her life. In her face. Twenty-four hours a day. She'd just opened her mouth and invited him in.

She winced. Book-wise and folk-foolish, her father used to describe her, a teasing twinkle in his eyes. And he was right. Jack's quiet, assured footsteps pursued her up the stairs. A less likely candidate for her compassion would be hard to find.

They reached the upper hall, its honey-colored balcony overlooking the vaulted living room and the massive stone fireplace.

"Did you know your sister was pregnant?" Jack asked.

Christina gathered her wandering thoughts. "Yes. My mother called me with the news."

"How is she doing?"

"Julia? I—her health is fine."

One dark eyebrow raised. "You talked to her recently?"

"No." She was faintly embarrassed. "There's an eleven hour time difference. It makes it difficult to keep in close touch."

He hitched his bag on his shoulder, regarding her steadily. "So, at eight in the morning here, it's seven at night there. Or aren't you an early riser?"

"I am a morning person, actually—not that it's any of your business. I just don't want Julia to feel I'm intruding."

"How could you be intruding? You're her sister."

Deep breaths. Eyes straight. "Her *younger* sister," Christina stressed. "Julia has always been something of a model in our family. For her to forget herself so far as to sleep with Kamal's son…"

"You think he forced her?"

The idea was horrible. But Jack's bluntness was in some way reassuring. "No. I did worry Julia was covering for him. An accusation of rape would certainly worsen the tension between our two countries. But Julia admitted to our mother that it was…consensual. A terrible moment of weakness, she said." Christina shook her head. "Knowing

Julia, she must feel so ashamed. I certainly wouldn't want her to think I'm judging her in any way."

"And you think by not calling her, she's going to feel better?"

Put that way…

"We're not that close," Christina said in excuse. "Not since we were children. Lucas was the one she—" But Christina's voice faltered. Lucas was gone.

"There's five years between my sister and me," Jack said quietly. "I always took care of her. She always looked up to me. But when I was wounded, after the operation, when I was stuck in the Navy hospital at San Diego sweating it through friction massage and all those damn range of motion exercises, my kid sister called every day. And I was never so damn glad to hear from anybody in my life."

Christina's heart wrenched at the poignant image of this tough, lean warrior confined to a bare, white room, dependent on the telephone to connect him to the world outside the hospital. But he didn't, couldn't, understand how insignificant her own role was within her family.

"This is different," she protested. "I wouldn't know what to say to her. Julia's always been so perfect. Our father actually asks for her advice. Even when her marriage ended a couple of years ago and there was this awful scandal, Julia always did the right thing. Said the right thing. And now, all because of some—"

Emotional meltdown.

Hormone storm.

"—error of judgment, everything she's been, everything she's worked for, is called into question. How can I possibly presume to counsel or comfort her?"

Particularly now, Christina thought miserably, when she

had Jack Dalton sleeping two doors down from her bedroom.

He stuck his thumbs in his belt loops, still watching her with those unreadable, slate-blue eyes. "Maybe you don't have to do either. Maybe you just have to let her know that you sympathize."

Oh, she sympathized, all right. She was terrified of making the same mistake herself.

Christina took another deep breath. Nonsense, she told herself stoutly. Jack Dalton was an experienced, disciplined warrior charged with her protection. He was not her family's enemy. He was not some smooth sexual predator or an opportunist out to sell torrid tales of his night in the royal love nest to the tabloids.

Christina refused to act like an uncertain, silly virgin who would blush and stammer and jump his big, lean body just because she had the chance.

All she had to do to keep control was to be distant and cool and polite.

"This is your room," she said, opening the door at the top of the stairs. "It has its own bath and phone. I hope you'll be very comfortable."

He looked briefly inside at the clean lines and warm tones of her guest room. His gaze lingered on the queen-size bed before he turned back to her. "Where do you sleep?"

She blushed and stammered, "I—my room is down the hall."

"Put me next to you."

Her heart stumbled. So much for distant. "Why?" she asked. Her tone managed cool and just missed polite.

"In case you need me in the night." He flashed her a wolf's grin. "If anything happens, I need to be where I can hear you. Reach you."

"But the room next to mine isn't as nice as this one."

"I can sleep anywhere. And I'm going to sleep better in your second-best guest room than I would lying across your doorway with my sword drawn."

He might sleep better, Christina thought ruefully.

She would be lucky to sleep at all.

Two hours later, she was tossing in her own four-poster bed, incapable of lying still and desperate not to make a sound. Her mattress creaked. She had never noticed it before. Why did she suddenly hear that small, betraying squeak now?

Because of him. Jack Dalton. She let her head fall—no, she let it down very slowly, very silently—onto her goose down pillow.

She could hear him through her walls—the sliding of drawers, the gurgle of pipes, the occasional creak of a footstep—and each unfamiliar sound cocooned her in unaccustomed and quite unintended intimacy.

She had lived alone for a long time.

Even in Montebello, Christina had had her own room, separate from her sisters'. During her years at UCLA, she'd had a condo off campus, with its own housekeeper and security. Dormitory life was judged "unsuitable" for a king's daughter. She certainly never shared an apartment, as so many other graduate students did.

A solitary child and a disciplined adult, Christina had always treasured her privacy. But now every tap and every thunk jarred her senses. Like a researcher in a lab, she was aware, alert, attuned to each new observation.

She heard the rattle of hangers and imagined him taking off his shirt. Water splashed, and she pictured his lean, bare back bending over the sink. He pulled out a chair, and the sound scraped her nerves. She remembered his clothes neatly folded on the chair in his hotel room and thought about his socks. Underwear. Boxers or briefs?

She buried her hot face in her pillow.

This was ridiculous.

It was arousing.

And it shook her to the core to realize that—just maybe—she had invited Jack Dalton into her house, into her life, not because he would keep her safe, not because he would let her retain control, not even because she sympathized with his struggle with his father's expectations.

She twisted around and stared sightlessly up at the high white ceiling. Maybe she had asked Jack simply because she wanted him around, blunt and experienced and unafraid.

And that was a much greater threat to her freedom than being kidnapped.

Pain sank fangs into Jack's shoulder and gnawed down his arm.

If he kept his eyes closed, maybe he could convince himself it was a dream. If he didn't move, maybe he could pretend the pain would go away.

Right. And maybe Princess Cupcake was going to glide into his bed and kiss him to make him feel better, but he doubted it.

The pain was nightmare real. And lying still was becoming as excruciating as movement would be.

He opened his eyes and took a cautious morning-after inventory, as if his own body were a stranger he'd picked up the night before and now was sorry he'd brought home. The shoulder joint ached. The scar felt tight enough to burst. He could count his pulse in throbs down his arm to his elbow and into his fingertips.

It would get worse if he exercised. That had been one

bitter lesson of the past five months. In SEALs, he could drive through the pain, push harder and farther and be rewarded with achievement and strength.

The therapist at the hospital had told him his reconstructed shoulder didn't work that way. If he overdid things, she explained, he would pay. He could actually make his injury worse.

At first he hadn't believed her.

And he'd paid.

Now he got up cautiously, in incremental stages. The pain would release him gradually as the day wore on, after ice and rest and a couple of the anti-inflammatory pills the docs had pushed on him. Until then, he was its captive.

He hated it.

But this morning, unlike all the other mornings, something beyond his own determination drove him out of bed. Christina was somewhere downstairs waiting. Waiting and—his head went up like a wolf's scenting the wind—brewing coffee?

He walked stiffly across the room, feeling a small satisfaction when he made it to the bathroom without jarring or tearing anything. But while he was washing his face, the pain came back, sneaky as a knife-wielding thug on a Colombian street, and sliced through his shoulder. He held on to the sink until it passed.

What made him think he was fit to look after a princess?

What made her think it?

He could barely lug a kid half a mile to the bus and still tie his own shoes the next morning.

He went downstairs in a state of snarling frustration that wasn't helped any by the sight of Christina, not a blond hair out of place, in ironed jeans and a silk T-shirt.

Her blue eyes widened when she saw him. He must look like hell.

"Good morning," she said, polite as a hostess in some toney restaurant. "May I get you some coffee?"

"Yeah. Thanks."

He sat at the kitchen table. The sun slanted over the trees and in through the wide windows, throwing rectangles of light onto the pale wood cabinets and gleaming white countertops. Christina reached into a cupboard for a mug.

As she stretched, her T-shirt cupped the full lower curves of her breasts. He watched, and to his generalized discomfort was added the localized ache of arousal.

She set his coffee in front of him and quickly backed away, as if he might bite. Maybe he would. "How do you feel this morning?"

"I've had hangovers that were worse. Of course, they were also a lot more fun to get."

"Don't try to distract me."

He wanted to. He didn't want her pity. "Is this some kind of girl thing? 'Tell me how you feel?'"

"Not at all," she said crisply. "It's a scientist thing. There's no value in ignoring facts. And based on the available evidence, I'd guess you are in pain."

She was sharp. Cute, too, with her face all free of makeup and her nose up in the air. And for all her claims of incompetence in the kitchen, she made a hell of a cup of coffee. He tried grinning at her. "Good guess."

"How *do* you feel?" she persisted, her eyes serious.

And he gave her a serious answer. "Like a damned banana."

She was momentarily diverted. "A banana?"

"Soft on the inside, soft on the outside," he explained. "The instructors call all SEAL trainees 'bananas' for the first few weeks of the training program."

A hint of a smile touched her lips. "So, how do we harden you up?"

He almost groaned. For all her intelligence, she was too innocent to know what she was asking. What she was inviting. He was plenty hard already.

"Ice," he said shortly. "Ice and rest."

Her pale brows lowered over her nose. "You should be in bed."

Now, there was an idea. A whole bunch of ideas, in fact. Think of the job, he ordered himself. Do the job.

"Not unless you join me," he said, deliberately blunt. "I'm supposed to stick with you, remember? Everywhere you go, I go."

Her skin turned faintly pink, but she didn't back down. "I'll be perfectly safe. I'm just working in the lab today."

"Then we'll go to the lab."

She went to the freezer. "You should rest. And I have work to do."

"So, do it. I told you I wouldn't interfere with your work."

"You'll be bored," she warned.

"Bored is good. Bored means nobody's shooting at you."

He saw her quick start and her quick recovery.

"Oh, very tough." She turned around and handed him a packed plastic bag. "Here's your ice."

It was hard not to admire a woman who dispensed aid without sympathy. Good thing she was royal, or he would have to consider marrying her.

He buried his face in his coffee mug. "Thanks," he mumbled.

She was ignoring him.

That was okay, Jack thought. That was part of the deal.

He didn't need to be the center of attention, and he meant what he'd said about letting her do her work.

But Christina had been going for almost four hours now, and it didn't seem quite fair that her work should absorb her so completely when his attention was so firmly fixed on her.

On her safety, he corrected himself.

The problem was that after he'd checked out the layout of the lab, there wasn't a hell of a lot for him to do. There was only one door in and out of the place, and windows that Christina said couldn't be opened because of potential contamination.

So maybe it was only natural that his attention was fixed on her, on her breasts under that baggy white lab coat, and her blue eyes narrowed with concentration. She got this little pleat between her eyebrows when she poured. Her face glowed from the heat of the gas burners. Or maybe it was from her being swaddled in that damn coat. He wasn't sure.

For most of the morning, she'd done the petri dish thing in the little room at the back of the lab. Now she was messing around with racks and racks of test tubes and some clear solution in a bottle.

At least the rest was doing his shoulder some good. But the inactivity left him bored. Restless. He fingered the camera in his pocket, but it seemed wrong to distract Christina while she was working. He slid off his stool and prowled around the long lab benches.

She looked up, annoyed. "Don't get too close. You could contaminate my dilution blanks."

It was an opening. He took it. "Your what?"

She lifted a test tube. "Saline. After I collect my soil samples, I need to dilute them to reduce the number of bacteria present."

"But you want the bacteria, right? So why would you dilute the samples?"

"A single gram of soil can contain over a trillion bacterial cells and an estimated twenty thousand different bacterial species. That's far too many to observe and record. The dilution blanks allow me to gradually reduce the number present in the sample and still reflect a proportional population of the bacteria."

He got that. He watched as she flamed and corked another test tube. "Why do you heat them up?"

"I'm sterilizing them."

He grinned. "And here I thought you just liked playing with fire."

He thought she might stammer, but she only angled her chin at him. "Maybe I do," she said. "I'm living with you, aren't I?"

And then he was the one in danger of falling over his tongue. Or swallowing it.

Before he could get his tongue working well enough to answer her, the lab door opened and some guy walked in.

Jack tensed, but the intruder didn't look dangerous. He was forty-something, tanned, dressed in all-natural fibers and good-looking in a beefy, blond, outdoorsy way that Jack instinctively resented.

"Who are you?" Jack demanded.

Offense flashed across the man's broad, handsome face.

Christina lowered her test tube. "Jack Dalton, Dr. Kevin Atkins. Jack, Dr. Atkins is assistant chair of our department."

Assistant chair was good, Jack thought. He wanted the guy to be a geek. Unfortunately, he didn't look like a geek any more than he looked like a terrorist. Maybe Montana didn't attract geek scientists.

"Nice to meet you," Atkins said with a wide, insincere smile. "Are you, um, visiting the university?"

"Actually, I'm visiting Christina," Jack drawled.

Atkins stiffened. "Really?"

"Jack is a friend of the family," Christina said. "From out of town."

"From out of town," Atkins repeated. "I hope you're enjoying your stay?"

He didn't come right out and ask where Jack was staying, but there was no doubt in Jack's mind that the question was there. Atkins hadn't made the mistake of standing close enough to Christina to contaminate her precious solution. But he was sending clear, proprietary male signals across the room: brushing back his already windblown hair, angling his body toward her, opening his jacket to rest his hands on his hips.

Christina didn't seem to notice. Any more than she'd noticed Jack all morning.

Jack bared his tooth in a wolf's grin. "Oh, yeah. I'm having a great time."

Atkins frowned. "Glad to hear it. Christina, do you have a copy of your notes for San Diego? I want to review your suggestions for bacterial inoculation in the field with regard to the department's efforts at the Running Creek station."

"Actually, I was planning to update my study. I'm going up to Big Lucky to see how my site plants are doing before I publish the results."

"When?" Atkins asked.

"I thought I'd leave tomorrow."

"Alone?"

"I…" Christina's shoulders straightened. *Uh-oh,* Jack thought. "That hasn't been decided yet."

"Why is it any of your business?" Jack asked.

Atkins turned on him the pinch-faced, academic version of the Royal Look. It was much more effective when Christina did it, Jack decided. "Department policy, Mr. Dalton," Atkins said. "Well, I should probably get back to my office."

"That would be good," Jack said.

After the assistant department chair left, Christina frowned at him. "You were rude."

He knew it, and it made him defensive. "I was doing my job. Protecting you."

"Kevin Atkins is no threat."

"He was hitting on you."

"He was not."

"Don't be fooled by the pipe and pleated khakis, princess. He has a major jones for you."

She shook her head. "Kevin doesn't smoke a pipe. Anyway, you led him to think that you were—that we are living together."

"We are."

"Not the way you implied."

He was starting to get angry, and that was good, that was better than feeling defensive or noticing how sexy clean she looked, with her smooth hair that would slip like water through his fingers, and her eyes blue and clear as the sea off the California coast, and a mouth that made him thirsty.

"So, you want me to wear a name tag now?" he asked. "'Hi, my name is Jack and I'm a bodyguard'?' You're the one who introduced me as a friend of the family."

"I didn't want him to believe there's a romantic connection."

"You worried he'll be jealous?"

She blinked at him with so much real surprise Jack felt

almost guilty. "Jealous? Of me? No. I'm not the type to inspire primal male behavior."

She wasn't just blind to Atkins. She obviously never looked in her own mirror.

"Why not?" Jack asked roughly. "You're female, breathing, not bad to look at."

"You find me attractive?" she asked carefully.

Her skepticism was insulting. "What, you think I'm only attracted to women whose bra size is bigger than their IQ?"

"Yes," she said.

Hell. But maybe it was better if she went on thinking that. Safer if she went on thinking that.

He shrugged. "You're not my type. That doesn't mean a *Town and Country* guy like Atkins wouldn't go for you."

And a woman like Christina deserved a guy like Atkins, he reasoned. A guy with the right clothes, who said the right things. A guy with a reliable job and two dependable arms. A guy who would appreciate all her class and not spend his time speculating on how warm and soft her breasts were or how her mouth tasted....

And if Atkins ever touched her, Jack thought grimly, he was a dead man.

"I see." Her voice was cool and blank as frosted glass. "Well, thank you very much for that revealing assessment."

She went back to her test tubes and left him with the uncomfortable feeling that he had screwed up. He just didn't know how. Or what to do to fix it. Or if he should even try.

It wasn't his assignment to make her feel good. *Don't go there, Flash.*

It was his job to keep her alive.

Chapter 6

Jack's posture, reclining against the cushions of her leather couch, was relaxed. But there was no softness at all to his flat, hard body, no give at all in his flat, hard voice.

"'Everywhere,' I said. That includes up the side of some godforsaken mountain so you can play in the mud."

Christina sighed and set her piece of pizza untasted on her Wedgwood plate. Why had she ever thought he would go along with what she wanted? No one else ever had. For all his big talk about not interfering, for all her foolish hope that after spending the day with her in the lab he would recognize or appreciate what she was doing, Jack didn't really respect her work at all. He was just like her father.

She felt a remembered sting. No, he was worse than her father. At least her father used to tell her she was pretty. Jack didn't even think she was attractive. *Not my type.*

In her usual, rational frame of mind, Christina might

have ascribed his callousness to pain or worry. Right now she just wanted him dead.

"I do not play in the mud," she said with icy precision. "I collect soil samples. And I do not want or need you along. You are still recovering from whatever wound you sustained, you cannot help with my research, and you will be in my way. I'll be perfectly safe."

"Camping alone in the mountains? Even assuming you're not kidnapped by terrorists, what if you fall off a cliff? Or get eaten by bears?"

She stuck out her chin. She had never seen a grizzly by Big Lucky, but black bears were fairly common. "I have more experience dealing with bears than you do."

"Do you have a gun?"

"No, but—"

"Whose stupid idea was this trip, anyway?"

Stung, she retorted, "Mine. It's my research. I've been invited to present a paper at a biology conference in San Diego, and I want to confirm my findings with the most recent data I can get."

"And your department actually allows you to go camping in the mountains alone?"

Christina stared down at the pizza. Mushroom on her side, pepperoni on his, and he'd made the delivery boy wait at the bottom of the walk. It was hard to fault him for his efforts to keep her safe. But his sarcastic tone set her teeth and her voice on edge. "I don't need departmental permission. I'm not a student any longer. And even if I were, it's only overnight. Everyone does it sometimes."

"And if everybody jumped off a cliff, would you do that, too?" Jack smacked his forehead with his hand. "God. I can't believe I said that. I sound like my father."

It was hard not to smile. But she managed it. "You sound like mine."

"Swell. That makes me feel better," he muttered.

Their eyes met. His were appalled and amused and wary. He looked so solid and real sitting there on her couch, with his hair sticking up and his day-old beard shadowing his jaw—six-feet-plus of solid, stubborn, edgy male. Her pulse kicked up. Her stomach lurched. She felt odd having him so close, living in her house, interfering in her life.

She was vulnerable to him.

She hated that.

She cleared her throat. "I guess you could come. If you're recovered tomorrow. Do you mind sleeping in a sleeping bag?"

His mouth quirked. "Princess, I can sleep standing up to my chin in water. I don't think an overnight in your Montana mountains is going to be a challenge."

Not for him, perhaps. He was a former U.S. Navy SEAL. He had experience she hadn't dreamed of.

But the thought of spending more time alone in very close quarters with Jack—hot, muscled, experienced Jack—made Christina shiver.

And it was too late to back out of the whole idea, because it was her danger, her project and her blind insistence that had landed her in this dilemma.

She straightened her spine. She was a Sebastiani. She would just have to make the best of things.

He would just have to make the best of things, Jack thought as Christina's truck bumped along the rutted road the next day. After all, it was his father, his assignment and his damn stubborn protective streak that had landed him in this mess.

Next to him, Christina drove with practiced assurance, her pale, long-fingered hands gripping the wheel. Her warmth reached across the seat. The truck smelled like her, like expensive soap and something else, something sweet and warm distilled from her own skin. Princess Cupcake. After being confined with her in the truck's small cabin all afternoon, he wanted to lick the icing right off her.

His body tightened.

Bad idea.

They had driven three hours along the interstate, from the university to the edge of the national forest, through a little town consisting of three bars, one schoolhouse and a gas station-convenience store. The pavement ended at the edge of town, and the truck churned up a mountain road.

Jack looked out at trees and shadows and rocky slopes. He was beginning to understand Christina's confidence now. It was hard to imagine kidnappers against this broad, empty backdrop of mountain and sky. Unless she happened to run into an encampment of wife-seeking survivalists. The thought made his jaw ache.

"Where are we?" he asked.

"Saturday Night Hill." Christina shifted gears as they rocked over a bump. "So called because the miners had so much trouble climbing back to their camps after celebrating in town on Saturday night."

"Miners? Like, gold miners?"

"The capital, Helena, was settled by gold miners." He got a kick out of the way her voice settled into lecturer's mode as competently and naturally as her truck changing gears. "But most of the hardrock mining in this area was copper and silver. There are thousands of adits from abandoned mines in these mountains. Big Lucky is a silver mine."

"So, what's the attraction for a biologist? Microbial ecologist," he corrected himself.

She slanted a look at him. "I don't want to bore you."

Did she think he was too dumb to get it? "Try."

"Well... Exposed to oxygen and water, the waste rock produced by the old mines forms acids that leach other metals from the ground and kill the vegetation. But in some areas, the plants are coming back. I want to know why."

"And you think it's bacteria?"

"Soil bacteria. Yes. There's actually a close symbiotic relationship between plants, fungi and bacteria. The trick is to identify and isolate the right mix of bacteria so that you could improve the plant communities in metal-contaminated areas."

He was impressed. "How did you get interested in this stuff?"

"You mean, what's a nice girl like me doing 'playing in the mud'?" she asked dryly.

She remembered. Did she mind?

"Okay, I was out of line with that one. I admit it. But you don't see your average princess out digging in the field or locked in a lab. Why do you do it?"

She was silent so long he figured she wasn't going to answer.

And that was fine. That was good. Who was he kidding? He didn't do sincere interest any better than he did commitment.

But then she said, "What else should I do? Lucas is—was—the heir." Her voice stumbled painfully. "Julia is the diplomat. Anna...well, Anna is the apple of our father's eye. I suppose at some point I decided I wanted to be something more than tabloid fodder."

"But why this?"

"Instead of hospital openings and palace tours?" She shrugged. "Quite simply, I find bacteria easier to understand than people. Besides..." She stopped.

"What?"

"There are mines in Montebello, too," she said, her chin lifting. "Maybe I like to think that in my own way I can contribute something to my country."

He looked at her again, really looked at her, at her porcelain-perfect profile and her lush, good-time girl mouth. But this time he didn't see some bright, spoiled royal escaping her duty. She was doing her duty. Contributing to her country with specialized training and dedication.

It was a concept any SEAL would understand.

"That's what you were talking about before," he said slowly. "Land reclamation strategies."

"Yes."

And he hadn't made the connection. He should have given her credit before this. Hell, her family should have given her credit.

"So, when your research is done, will you go home?"

She hesitated. "I'm not sure. My research is fairly open-ended. And I may not be the most effective person to implement my strategies in Montebello."

"I figure you'd at least want to visit."

"Oh, really? And when was the last time you went home to Texas?"

From another woman, that sideways look would have been flirting. Not from Christina, though. She was too smart to get mixed up with a guy like him. Still, the challenge in that smiling glance made Jack's mouth go dry and his mind go blank.

He worked his mouth. Kick-started his brain. Talk to her, moron. Talking was safer than thinking...what he was thinking. *Don't go there, Flash.* "It's been a couple of years. Anyway, it's different for me than for you."

"Why?"

"Well, you've still got family at home. My sister married and moved away."

"What about your father?"

On the other hand, talking had dangers of its own. She was already on his mind. Under his skin. He didn't need her digging into his psyche as well.

She was a job, he reminded himself.

Not his buddy.

Not his girl.

Not his latest or his next screw.

Only in fairy tales and porno flicks did the royal princess get it on with the hired muscle. He was just her bodyguard, and she was just a stopgap paycheck, a hedge against toxic boredom, while he figured out what to do with his life now that his career had blown apart.

He said, dismissively, "My old man hated hanging around home. Maybe I take after him more than I knew."

"But—"

She was too close. He cut her off. "How long till we get to this campsite?"

"Ten minutes, no more."

He'd managed to put the reserve back in her voice, he thought, relieved and sorry. Her pretty lips pressed together, and she drew herself up on the truck's padded bench like it was some fancy gilded parlor chair. The movement brought his attention to those high, firm, round breasts. Jack hadn't been so fixated on a female's breasts since Darlene Johnson made the cheerleader squad in eighth grade.

Disgusted with himself, he slumped against the passenger door and waited out the rest of the ride in grim silence.

Well, for pity's sake, what had she done wrong now?

One minute they were amicably discussing her work and his family, and the next minute he was glowering at her as if she had just poked him with a sharp stick.

Christina stifled a sigh and concentrated on pounding in the next tent peg. They had argued over that as well, Jack insisting that securing shelter was *his* responsibility and Christina pointing out that it was *her* tent and she was perfectly capable of putting it up herself. She had won that round. But her victory hadn't eased any of the tension between them.

Clearly, she had been alone in the lab too long. Otherwise she wouldn't be so flattered, so flustered, by male attention. She would know what to say—or what not to say—to keep a conversation going.

Or better still, she wouldn't care.

She pounded harder. After all, Jack was the one who had encouraged her to talk. He hadn't once given her any sign that he was bored. And so she had allowed the novelty of his unfamiliar, focused interest to tempt her from behind her barriers.

Yes, and then he'd left her in the open with her emotions hanging out. The hammer bounced off the peg and hit the side of her foot. Christina winced. Never again.

She stood awkwardly. Behind her, Jack had finished unloading the truck and was hauling their food supplies up on a bear pole. With one hand. Because of his shoulder? Sympathy pinched her.

Don't be foolish, she scolded herself. He didn't want her sympathy. He didn't want anything to do with her. She was just a job to him.

"Food or fuel?" he asked.

She frowned. "What?"

He secured the knot. Single-handed, she noticed, and tried not to be impressed. He was a sailor. It stood to reason he would be good at knots.

"We'll eat faster if we work as a team," he explained

evenly. "I don't know your strengths yet, so I'm asking. Do you want to fish or collect firewood?"

At least he had asked her preference this time instead of automatically taking the hunter-gatherer role.

"I can do either one," she said.

He nodded. "I'll fish," he said, so promptly she suspected he had an idea of her strengths, after all.

To tease him, she asked, "Would you like a rod, or are you planning on scooping trout out of the water with your bare hands?"

"I'll take the tackle. Unless you want me to use a safety pin and my belt webbing."

She blinked. Was he serious? But she went to get the collapsible rod and reel from her pack.

"Thanks." Jack took the rod in his left hand and reached smoothly behind his back with his right. "We should both have the proper equipment."

And he pulled out a gun. A short, smooth, black gun. He turned it over in his hands and then extended it to her, butt first, muzzle pointing to the ground.

Christina's heart jumped into her throat. She swallowed hard. "I don't want it."

"You need it. You see anything suspicious, fire a shot in the air. Anything dangerous, shoot to stop."

"I can't."

"Look, if you aim for an arm or a leg, you're likely to miss. The body presents the biggest target."

"No, I mean...I don't know how to shoot."

He studied her, his navy blue eyes expressionless. And then he set down the fishing rod. "This is a Glock. It's pretty fault-tolerant. The safety is here. You have to release it like this, see?" He held the barrel to demonstrate. "Don't take the safety off unless you're going to fire."

He slipped around behind her. His chest was warm and

close against her back. Her heart raced. Adrenaline, she told herself firmly. She was reacting to the gun.

The gun, and Jack.

His right arm extended along hers. He raised them together.

"Bring your arm up like this," he said in her ear. "Point your shoulder to the target. You squeeze the trigger. Don't pull. Be prepared for it to kick. I'll hear it, and I'll come running."

She looked along their arms to where his big brown hand covered hers on the gun. Her stomach quivered. "Can't I just scream instead?"

He stepped away from her. "A scream won't stop an attacker."

She turned to face him, the unaccustomed weight of the gun dragging her arm down. "But it would bring you."

His eyes gleamed. "Sure. But you don't strike me as a screamer, princess. Take the gun."

She flushed. She thought she understood his words, but she didn't trust that tone. "Where do I put it?"

"As long as you've got the safety on, you can carry it in your jacket pocket."

It was a gauntlet. A dare. *You don't strike me as a screamer, princess.* His challenge moved her where her own danger did not.

She put the gun in her pocket.

It stayed there. She felt it, grazing against her hip as she walked, knocking against her side when she stooped to drag deadfall from the underbrush, a distracting, alien presence.

She tried to find escape in the familiar task and wild surroundings. She liked being alone in this forest, the only chatter from the squirrels, the only whispers from the wind.

She took joy in the fleeting fellowship of the birds, the silent company of the dignified stands of spruce and fir and lodgepole pine. Snow still slept in shade-protected banks, but in the clearings the ground pulsed with delicate color and life, paintbrushes, lupines and shooting stars.

She breathed it all in—the solitude, the wildness, the peace.

But like the smell of smoke, the awareness of Jack hovered at the edges of her senses. The gun pulled at her coat pocket, an unwelcome reminder of danger. He tugged at her thoughts, disturbing her calm.

She ought to resent it.

She ought to resist him.

But while she knelt at their campsite, coaxing the fire to life, Jack appeared, moving as silently as one of the mountain lions that still hunted these hills. He stepped out of the trees and into the fire circle like a Shoshone warrior stepping out of the past.

And her heart, her guarded, regulated, lonely heart, quickened at the sight of him.

"You built a good fire," he said, coming toward it.

"I was hoping you'd cook on it," she said, as lightly as her rapidly beating heart allowed.

He held up a string of fish—two cutthroats and a brook trout—in answer.

"You're good," she said.

His smile started in his deep-set eyes. "I'm experienced."

Her breath faded. Oh, my. Oh, dear.

Oh, for pity's sake. What was the matter with her? Fishing. The man was talking about fishing.

"That gives you an advantage over me, then."

He shrugged. "Sometimes experience is an advantage. Sometimes you just get lucky."

That didn't sound like he was talking about fishing. She stood to dig the frying pan out of her pack.

She thought another man might try to take advantage of their isolation, the spurious intimacy of setting up camp together, to force a different kind of intimacy. In fact, six years ago, another man had. But she hadn't thought Jack was that kind of man.

For all of her advanced degrees, she thought painfully, sometimes she could be really dumb.

She straightened her spine. "And are you planning to get lucky twice in one night?"

"Not unless you're still hungry after dinner." He grinned. "Things get pretty treacherous after dark. I'd hate to stumble around trying to satisfy you."

Her face flamed. Her voice dripped icicles. "I suppose you think I'm naive."

He looked at her. Frowned. And squatted on his heels beside the fire.

"No," he said seriously, all teasing gone. The scent and sizzle of frying fish rose in the air. "I think you're careful. And that's good. That makes my job easier."

His job.

This was a job to him.

She was a job to him.

She had to remember that.

And really, Christina thought later as they banked the fire for the night, she would rather be a job to Jack than some gullible girl he felt he had to sleep with to make points with her father. Or get his picture in the tabloids. Or win bragging rights in the graduate student lounge for making it with a real live princess.

Memory burned a hole in her chest. Her eyes stung. Smoke, she told herself, and blinked fiercely.

"You all right?" Jack asked.

Chin up, eyes straight, she gave him her best plastic princess smile. "Of course. Why?"

He stood, brushing his big hands against his thighs. She looked away. "Because I know you've got to find this a little awkward."

"Find what awkward?"

"This. Us."

It was his job to look after her. But all the same, she was touched by his unexpected consideration for her feelings. "No more awkward for me than for you."

"I think it is. I'm used to sharing a tent with five other guys. I bet you're not."

Her heart tripped in panic. Not five. Not even one. But if he could be professional about this, so could she.

"I'll manage," she said stiffly.

"Right." He looked across the fire at her. Its banked heat danced in his eyes. "Time to turn in, then," he drawled.

Chapter 7

During Hell Week, Jack had snatched scant hours of sleep huddled on a bare cot by the ocean. Even freezing, aching and strung out, he'd fallen asleep in short order.

He was warm now, and dry. Instead of sharing a tent with five wet, shivering, sand-chafed and exhausted men, he had a gorgeous blonde breathing beside him.

And he'd never had so much trouble dropping off in his life.

He stared at the nylon roof slanting two feet over his head and listened to Christina shift and sigh. His back ached from contact with the hard ground, but he wasn't rolling over. No, sir. In the tight confines of the tent, her sleeping bag already brushed his. Her breath stirred the air by his cheek. The temperature in the tent rose a few uncomfortable degrees. Inside his sleeping bag, under his clothes, he was hard and ready as an M-16.

He needed sex.

He wanted her.

He wasn't getting what he needed tonight.

He had a job to do—a job already complicated by the sexual tension that pulsed between them. It would be damn near impossible if he frightened her or forfeited her trust.

Christina's family was threatened. Her freedom was curtailed by the possibility of a terrorist kidnapping. The last thing she needed was to have the man charged with the responsibility of keeping her safe start poking at her.

She stirred and sighed again.

Keep your mouth shut, he thought. Let her think you're sleeping. Easier that way on both of them.

He could smell her sweet soap scent and the tang of wood smoke in her hair. If he reached out, if he rolled over, he could touch it. Touch her.

"Trouble falling asleep?" he asked the nylon over his head. *Hell, Dalton. Can't you keep your trap zipped?*

She cleared her throat, an endearing, intimate sound in the dark. "A little," she admitted.

"Close quarters."

"Yes. It's a small tent." Another silence fell, measured by the throb of his pulse. "Perhaps if we changed position we would be more comfortable?" she offered.

Yeah. Like she could crawl on top.

"What did you have in mind?" he asked.

"It might be easier if we weren't…face-to-face?"

He was already lying on his back. "So, turn over."

"I can't," she confessed in a small voice. "I can only sleep if I'm on my left side."

Facing him. Her breath in his ear, her knees touching his hip… His brain flamed at the images.

"Well, I can't sleep on my right side," he said harshly, "so we're stuck."

"Oh, your shoulder." Her contrition flowed across the little space separating them, tugging at his resolution like knee-high surf. He actually got the impression that she'd forgotten about his injury. But then she spoiled things by asking, "How is it today?"

"It's fine."

"Do you need ice?"

Not for his shoulder. "I'm fine."

"How did—you were wounded four months ago?"

Jack frowned. Had he told her that?

He never talked about the shooting, not to the docs, not to his sister, not even to the members of the team. Especially not to the team. But yeah, in his hotel room, sitting on his bed, he'd said something to Christina.

"You really want to talk about this now?" he asked.

"I'm just trying to make conversation to help us both get to sleep."

"Oh, yeah, that will absolutely do it. Let's talk about how my shoulder got blown to bits and my career got shot to hell. Very relaxing."

"All right," Christina conceded. "Not good bedtime story material. I agree. Tell me what you want to do now."

Her voice was quiet and matter-of-fact, neither slick with pity nor thick with curiosity. And he liked it, damn it. Liked the way she respected his boundaries without skulking in retreat. Liked the way she stood up to him without ever pulling rank.

He liked too damn much about her.

"I want to get my full range of motion back. But that's not going to happen."

"Why not? If it's only been four months—"

"The bullet did too much soft tissue damage."

"They can't repair it?"

"They tried. The docs moved a muscle flap from my back to my shoulder."

"It didn't work?"

"It worked. At least I have a shoulder now. I'm supposed to be grateful for that."

"But...?" she prompted, probing for answers like the scientist she was.

He should have felt flayed. Dissected. But something in her calm, precise voice allowed him to face the facts. Forced him to face the facts. "But the scar will always be stiff, and my arm extension over my head will always be limited."

"They made you resign," she said carefully.

"No. I could stay in the navy. The navy always needs good technicians. But the SEALs...the Teams need warriors. I couldn't—can't—be a SEAL anymore."

And that's all he'd ever wanted to be.

The best of the best.

Like his father.

"But you are still serving your country's interests."

"I'm not defending my country anymore, princess. I'm protecting you."

"You are protecting the stability of Montebello," she told him firmly. "And I am grateful."

He didn't want her gratitude any more than he wanted her pity. He was no hero. And lying with her here in the darkness, her warm body and her cool voice and the sweet, expensive smell of her, he was having some definitely unheroic thoughts. "I thought you didn't want a bodyguard."

"I didn't. I don't. But if I must have one, I am glad that it is you."

Jack clenched his teeth. Didn't she know what she was inviting with that soft affirmation? No, of course she didn't. She was too damn innocent.

"So, you're finally doing what your daddy wants," he stated, deliberately goading. She was inches away. He was dying.

"We both are," she retorted. "At least I'm prepared to make the best of the situation."

"You want me to make the best of this situation?"

"I think you should try."

"Fine," Jack snapped, and rolled toward her.

His hand tangled in her wood smoke scented hair, and he found her mouth in the dark.

Shock crashed through Christina.

This was no tender first kiss. She might be as unawakened as Sleeping Beauty, but Jack was no Prince Charming. He was a large, experienced, angry man.

And he was aroused. Even she could tell that.

His mouth moved over hers, hungry and hot. His hands gripped her shoulder, her hair. She felt the tiny sting against her scalp and arched her neck.

Jack made a deep sound and buried his lips against her throat. Assaulted by sensation, she could barely breathe. His breath was so hot. His hands were so urgent. His hair, brushing her jaw, was so impossibly soft. He moved again, roughly aligning their bodies, and even through the thickness of their sleeping bags she could feel his heavy strength, the power in his chest, the hard bulge between his thighs.

Oh, glory. She gasped, and he took advantage of her open lips to possess her mouth again. His tongue stroked hers. Excitement quivered through her. But before she could begin to respond with tentative touches of her own, he thrust his tongue deeper, intent on having, taking, proving…something.

In her inexperience, she could not keep up with him. She could only wonder and absorb and hold on.

He kissed her, long, wet, hot kisses that left her drained and shaking. His hand moved up and closed over her breast, and she welcomed his touch, just as she welcomed the thrust of his tongue, the jut of his hips. Her nipples tingled and tightened. The swamp of sensation was bewildering. Indecent. Wonderful.

She arched and wriggled under him, trying to get closer to his hardness and his heat, frustrated by his weight and the bulky sleeping bags. She opened her eyes, trying to see him in the dark, trying to make images and sense out of the swirling chaos inside her.

But the darkness defeated her. Her own body defeated her. He touched her again, his palm sure and hard and exciting against her breast, and she moaned.

He froze. His hand froze.

And then he growled a curse and rolled off her, breathing hard.

She lay where he left her, oddly bereft. Her heart hammered against her ribs. She wondered if he could hear it. She could hear him, hear the harsh rasp of his breathing.

Do something, she ordered herself. Say something.

"What was that?" she asked, hoping he would tell her what he felt. Hoping he could give her some clue about how to deal with her own new, confusing jumble of emotions and sensations.

"That," he said heavily, "was a mistake."

She felt numb. "A mistake."

"Yeah. Don't worry. It won't happen again."

She moistened her lips. "Why not?"

"Because it's completely inappropriate, that's why."

"Because of my rank?" she asked carefully.

He had to help her understand. She *needed* to understand. Her body still protested the loss of his. She was cold, despite the swaddling layers of her sleeping bag and her thick socks.

"Because of your inexperience."

Well. Yes. Her inexperience was painfully apparent to

her. Obviously, it was apparent to him as well. Hurt tightened her chest. She hadn't known what to do during his
hot, hard, almost desperate kiss. And she didn't know what
to do now.

"Should I apologize?" she asked coolly.

A short laugh escaped him. "Hell, no. I'm supposed to
do that. After you slap my face."

"I wouldn't dream of doing anything so cliché." Although she would have liked to take the frying pan he'd
used to cook their dinner, and hit him over the head with
it. How dare he kiss her nearly senseless and then stop?
She felt like crying. She didn't, of course.

She said, very stiffly, "But I accept your apology."

"Swell."

She flinched. But in the darkness he did not see.
"Would you prefer that I sulk? Or should I scream at
you?"

"No." Jack rubbed his face with his hand. Damn, she
was a cool one. Except when he kissed her. When he
kissed her, she was hot. Exciting. Perfect.

And innocent, he reminded himself. She was innocent.
It was his job to protect her.

His jaw clenched. "Look, if you had any idea— But
you don't. And I'm not getting paid to teach you."

"Well, I certainly wouldn't want you to do anything
that's not in your contract," she said in that clipped, precise way that pushed all his dominant-male buttons.

He said, through his teeth, "We don't have a contract."

"You're right. We don't. We don't really have anything,
do we? What a good thing that you stopped."

A good thing. Yeah.

Jack wanted her to believe that. Because as he tried to
force his restless body to sleep, he was having a tough
time convincing himself.

* * *

Christina wrapped her cold hands around her hot mug of coffee and stared at the surface, chalky with powdered milk. If she didn't make eye contact with Jack, grouchy and competent on the other side of the fire, she could get through this.

"I want to apologize if I made you uncomfortable last night," she said.

She got a sense of movement, abruptly checked. "What?"

Her hands tightened until her palms burned. She could get through this. She *would* get through this. Honor demanded it.

"Last night," she repeated. "When I kissed you. I realize that you are not in my employ, but you do nonetheless report in some fashion to my father, and I'm sure my…my overtures put you in an awkward position."

There. She'd said it. She could be satisfied.

But Jack, apparently, was not impressed.

He straightened, tall and dark and rough-looking with a day's beard on his jaw and his hair sticking up from sleep. Her heart beat faster.

"First off, princess, you didn't kiss me. I kissed you." He jerked his cup, and the dregs of his coffee spattered into the bushes. "Second, I was uncomfortable, but not in the way you mean. Last night, I was hot for you. Hard. Turned on. But that's my problem, not yours. You've got nothing to apologize for."

She knew better. His blunt words made her shiver. She could barely believe they were having this discussion. But she was responsible for starting it. Just as, last night, she had been responsible for his condition.

Hot. Hard. Turned on.

Her breath caught in excitement. Oh, for pity's sake. She was reacting like an idiot.

She lifted her chin. "Yes, so you said. But I disagree. The situation would be much less awkward if I hadn't overreacted." Her cheeks were burning, and not from the warmth of the fire. She stared into the flames, confessing, "I've never been so forward with a man in my life."

"That wasn't forward."

She would not let him absolve her. "It felt very forward to me. I'm not that sort of person. Compared to the rest of my family, I'm not a warm, physical person at all."

"What does that mean?"

She shrugged, not sure how to explain her difference from the rest of the close-knit, loving Sebastianis. "Papa and Anna are both very passionate. Lucas, too." But she could not bear to talk about her brother, whose wild streak had led to his being lost in the Colorado mountains. "Mother says it's their hot Italian blood. Mother is much more restrained—she was a governess to the Windsors before she married, did you know that?—but always very loving and devoted. Julia takes after her. Not that they would do anything improper, you understand, but the media is always catching them in little public displays of affection."

Speaking of her family brought them vividly back to her. She swallowed an ache of longing for her blond, loving mother, for the queen's unabashed affection and natural confidence. The king of Montebello had pursued the former governess long and publicly before she succumbed to his suit.

What would she say if she knew her daughter had been ready to give up her virginity to a sailor she'd known less than forty-eight hours?

"What about you?" Jack asked.

"Oh." Embarrassed, Christina ducked her head, sipping her coffee. "I'm not a hugger. Not a toucher. That's probably why I reacted so inappropriately last night."

"I didn't say that. I said you were inexperienced."

"Perhaps I just need more experience, then," she said lightly, and held her breath.

"Not with me," Jack said bluntly.

Ouch. No, of course not. That would be too *inappropriate* for Senior Chief Do-My-Duty Dalton.

"I wasn't suggesting I get my experience with you."

His eyes narrowed. "In case you haven't noticed, princess, I'm the only man around."

He was also the only man she had ever wanted.

She resented that, resented him for making her feel all the deficiencies of her sheltered, tabloid-shy existence.

"But not the only man I know," she said.

"Oh, right. You think Atkins can give you what you want?"

She hadn't thought about Kevin Atkins at all. "You were the one who said he was interested."

"Forget it. He's all wrong for you."

She raised haughty eyebrows. "Is he worse for me than you are?"

No, he wasn't. Damn. Jack hated that. In fact, the assistant chair of her department, with his blond good looks and his smooth good manners and his string of academic credentials, was probably as close to perfect for her as any man within a radius of, say, a thousand miles.

"The point is, you should be concentrating on your safety," Jack said doggedly.

Christina's spine straightened. She looked at him as if he were a not particularly interesting specimen under her microscope. Frustration boiled in his veins. He wanted to yank her into his arms and kiss her until she cried out his name.

"I think a better objective would be for me to concentrate on my work," she said.

"Right," Jack said. He could feel his jaw tighten. If he ground his teeth any harder, he'd break a molar. "You do that. We'll both do that."

They struck camp in near silence. Their breath made soft clouds in the morning air, but the temperature on the mountain was nothing compared to the royal chill rolling off Christina.

She didn't shirk the work, though, Jack noticed with reluctant admiration. She rolled, packed and carried with the graceful efficiency of a practiced camper. And she tackled their hike at a pace that would have left the last woman he'd dated—Krystal, the aerobics instructor from Galveston—gasping.

Following behind Christina on the trail, Jack shook his head over the contradictions of her. Her pale hair was pulled back in a simple braid. She wore boots and jeans and layers of shirts. But there was no mistaking the regal tilt to her head, no disguising the wickedly female body under the androgynous clothes. When the sun cut through the pines to drench her strong, clean face and fine textured skin in light, she was so beautiful his breath stopped.

Christina stopped, too.

For an uneasy second Jack wondered if he'd been dazed enough, dumb enough, to actually say something out loud. But she only unstrapped a steel tube from her pack, hollow on one end, with a handle on the other, and dropped to her knees in the dirt and vegetation.

"Where are we?" he asked.

She didn't look at him. "We're coming into the Big

Lucky mine tailings. I'll take samples here, and compare them with samples from closer to the mine."

She pulled a brown jug from the pack and unscrewed the top. A sharp smell cut the cool air. Jack identified it. Ethanol. Christina dipped the end of her tool into the jug and then lit it with a cigarette lighter. Blue flame danced eerily along the steel.

"Does Smokey know you're doing this?" Jack asked.

She lifted her blond brows in question.

"'Only you can prevent forest fires,'" he intoned.

Her lips curved. But she responded primly. "The probe needs to be sterilized. Otherwise I might transfer bacteria from one site to another."

She settled to her work with the pure-minded focus of a nun. Or a soldier, he thought. She looked like Joan of Arc kneeling in a drift of wildflowers, purple spires and bright pink trumpets brushing her jeans.

He wanted her. Or at least, he wanted this image of her—her pale, narrow hands, her soft, absorbed mouth, the sunshine like a blessing on her hair. He eased his little Nikon camera from his jacket pocket.

He focused and shot as Christina used a narrow spatula to scoop dirt from the probe into a small plastic bag, her face serious and intent. Got another as she squeezed out the air and rolled the bag closed.

She printed something on the front. "Would you mind—" She saw his camera and frowned. "I told you I don't like having my picture taken."

He could tell her to get over it, but he didn't want to tick her off. "I hate to break it to you, princess, but you're not the only scenic view around here."

She sat back on her heels, taking in the panorama of rocks and trees and sky, and then she looked him in the eye for maybe the first time all morning and smiled. "It is beautiful, isn't it?"

"Sure is." Okay, so he wasn't talking about the scenery, but a guy could be forgiven a little deception when he was reeling from the full force of that smile.

"Do you think you could take a photo for me? Of the site, I mean?"

"Sure. Why?"

"It might be effective to have slides to go with my presentation."

"This isn't slide film. But yeah, I can get you some pictures." He fiddled with the camera. If he had a wider lens...

"I don't want to impose."

He shrugged and framed a shot. "I've got nothing better to do. Unless Smokey's cousins decide to pay us a visit and I have to protect you from Mama Bear."

"It's not that the data itself isn't convincing," Christina argued. He wondered who she was working so hard to persuade. He was with her all the way. "But a visual comparison of the sites—"

"It's okay. I get it. Pictures are sexy."

She actually flushed. Because he'd used the word *sexy?* Oh, man. She *was* innocent. And he was in deep, deep trouble here.

She did the princess angle with her chin. "Sexy things appeal to you?"

She appealed to him. Too much. "I meant, pictures will create a connection with the audience. Bring them closer. That's what you want them for, right?"

"Is that what you use them for?"

"It's what most people use them for. Capture the moment. Keep your memories." He squeezed off another shot of flowers. "How many pics do you want?"

"Some from each site. When did you start taking pictures?"

"When I was sixteen." The year his mama had died. "The yearbook advisor handed me a camera and told me to make myself useful."

Good old Mrs. Wermuth, with her orange lipstick and her Certs-scented breath and her sharp compassion. Her exact words to the sullen troublemaker in her class had been, "Time you made something of yourself, boy, besides a problem."

He owed her. Eight or nine years ago he'd gone back to Boone High to explain his debt, only to find out the old English teacher had died. But every time he developed a roll of film, he remembered her and was grateful.

"High school yearbook? Very glamorous," Christina said dryly.

"Oh, yeah. Almost as glamorous as taking pictures for the navy."

"You said you took intelligence pictures."

She had a good memory. "Not initially. I started out taking PR and simulated battle shots for navy files." He pulled a face, remembering. "I got razzed about it, too, when I started BUD/S."

"Razzed?"

He shrugged. "Being a PM, a photographer's mate, is kind of like being an accountant. You don't get a lot of respect from the glory boys. You know how most SEALs get a nickname in training?"

She shook her head. Her attention went to his head like bourbon.

"Well, they do," he said. "Mine was Flash."

Her brow pleated as she worked that one out. "As in flashbulb?"

He grinned. "Yeah. Also Jack Flash. Flash in the pan. Flash, to, uh, expose oneself."

Her eyes dropped briefly to the front of his jeans. His body reacted as if she'd touched him. "I see. I mean, I'm sure that was very hard for you. *Difficult* for you," she corrected swiftly.

"I got over it," he drawled.

Her face was pink. "I'm sure you put your talents to good use."

"Yeah. Surveillance shots, after-action reports and the C.Y.A."

"What is C.Y.A.?"

"The Cover Your Ass file. A record of what really went down on every mission, all nice and documented so that if the brass ever decided to rewrite history, they couldn't make us the goats."

"You used pictures you took to—to blackmail your superior officers?" Disapproval chilled her voice.

He scowled. "I used pictures for a lot of things, cupcake. Including protecting my career and my team. Sometimes pictures are all you've got to show how things really are."

"And sometimes pictures lie. Things—people—aren't always what they are made to appear."

Wasn't that the truth.

Look at him. With his shirt on, all his scars were hidden, the ones on his shoulder and the ones he didn't talk about. He looked like the Navy SEAL he used to be.

Look at her. With her face free of makeup, and mud on her knees, Christina looked like any other...no.

Jack started to sweat. Because whatever she wore, Christina was still herself, always herself, all of her selves: the princess who looked like her tiara gave her a headache; the *Sports Illustrated* version of the Lady of the Lake; the intent, absorbed scientist; the hot mouth in the dark. He couldn't see one face of her anymore without seeing all the others.

Oh, yeah. Deep, deep trouble here.

To protect her, he needed her to remain a job. To protect himself, he needed to see her as a job. He was used to lining up his shots. Controlling his angles. Establishing his distance with his lens.

Yeah, big shot Flash Dalton.

He hadn't counted on meeting the one woman who could break the frame.

Chapter 8

Christina's lips compressed as she drew one milliliter of solution into a pipette and added it to a fresh dilution blank. It was boring and exacting work.

And it didn't help her concentration at all that what she really wanted to do was upend the entire rack of test tubes over Jack Dalton's head.

His deep voice echoed in her brain. *That was a mistake. I'm not getting paid to teach you.*

Dolt. Boor.

She drew a deep breath. She did not have time for this...this distraction. She had packed her samples in snow for the drive home and transferred them to petri dishes as soon as they arrived at the lab. But for her work to have any validity at all, she needed to get the bacteria under a microscope soon. Now.

And the heck with Jack Dalton.

He lounged against the lab bench just outside the sterile

room, his long legs stretched in front of him, his hard face impassive.

"How much longer will this take?" he asked.

"As long as I need," she snapped, and for some stupid reason that made him grin.

"Don't get touchy. I don't mind it when a woman needs more time."

She was tired of trying to understand him. She was tired, period, and her head ached, and he'd hurt her feelings.

She began to speak slowly, with exaggerated patience, as if she were addressing a class of not very bright third graders. "Bacteria reproduce very rapidly. Whole populations can change within hours in a laboratory setting. I need to make as many observations as I can tonight."

He stopped looking smug and looked annoyed instead. She was glad. Why should she be the only one suffering? "Thank you for that explanation, princess. But you missed my point. Most snatches take place in the late afternoon or evening, when people are coming off work and off guard. I wanted to know if you were following a schedule somebody else would know."

She closed her eyes briefly. Just what she needed to feel better. A reminder that she was a target of terrorist kidnappers.

"No schedule," she said.

It was almost a relief when Kevin Atkins walked into the lab. At least he regarded her as a mind, as a colleague, and not as a *mistake*.

"Christina?" He smiled, managing to look boyishly disheveled and bookish all at once. *He's got a major jones for you,* Jack jeered in her head. "Have you got a minute?"

"Not really, Kevin." She smiled to soften her refusal.

"I have a lot to finish up before the San Diego conference."

"That's just what I want to talk with you about," Kevin said.

Jack had crossed his arms against his chest. Propped against the black slate table, he listened, his face sardonic.

She ignored him. "Unfortunately, it will have to wait," she told Kevin. "If I don't get to these samples tonight…"

"Of course. I understand." And he really did; that was the nice thing about him. One of many nice things about him, she told herself firmly. He was a careful researcher and a zealous advocate for land restoration. They had interests and associates in common. He was a known quantity.

If she suddenly decided to throw away a lifetime of caution and find out what she'd been missing with the male of the species, Kevin Atkins would be a safe place to start.

Kevin Atkins was boring, whispered a rebellious voice inside her. It sounded like Jack's.

"Stop that," she whispered back.

Kevin looked surprised. "Stop what?"

She flushed. "Sorry. I'm a little—" Tired. Frustrated. "—distracted."

Kevin smiled, the sun lines at the corners of his eyes crinkling attractively. "Another time, then." He hesitated. His gaze slid to Jack and back again. "Perhaps over dinner? Tomorrow?"

That would show him, Christina thought militantly. Show him what, exactly, she wasn't sure, but then she really was tired. And distracted.

"Dinner sounds lovely," she said.

Kevin looked even more surprised. She felt a moment's unease. Was she supposed to play hard to get? But then he said, "Great. Seven o'clock okay?"

She nodded.

"Great," he repeated. He adjusted the lapels of his tweed jacket. "Well. Tomorrow, then. I'll pick you up."

"Do you need my address?"

"It's in your file."

She nodded again. Kevin opened his mouth, hesitated and then walked out.

"You want to tell me what that was about?" Jack asked.

She raised another test tube, pleased when her hands and voice both remained steady. "It was fairly self-explanatory, I thought. Kevin invited me to dinner."

"I hope he picks someplace with decent food."

"I'm sure he will. Kevin entertains a great deal in support of the environment—ranchers, senators…. But it's nice of you to be concerned about my evening."

"I'm concerned about mine."

She lowered the test tube, a horrible suspicion forming in her mind. "You are not coming."

"Sure am. Everywhere you go, I go."

"Not on a business dinner!"

"Everywhere. You think the daughter of the president turns down Secret Service protection when she goes out?"

"That's different."

"Yeah, it is. As far as I know, she's not getting threatening letters in the mail."

She changed tactics. "I thought you'd be grateful to have a night off."

"You want gratitude? Stay home."

"Kevin Atkins is the assistant chairman of this department. I am not breaking a date with him because you have a problem with it."

"So, it's a date now?"

She blinked. "What?"

Jack uncrossed his arms. Took a step toward her. "You

called it a date. Before, you said it was a business dinner. Which is it?''

Her head throbbed. Her heart pounded. ''What possible difference does it make to you?''

He held her gaze for a long, steady minute. ''None at all, I guess.''

Saturday night. Date night at Fayrene's Steakhouse.

The hostess, wearing a crisp white apron and a short black skirt, led the way through the dark dining room to their table. Christina looked around curiously.

Not many students, she saw. This was an older crowd: serious couples and stranded business types, all determined to have a good time in a small town on a Saturday night. A piano and a fiddle squeezed in beside the tiny dance floor, where a few brave souls scraped and bumped together.

The hostess stopped beside a high-backed booth and flashed them a smile as closely calculated as a gratuity. ''Roger will be with you shortly to take your drink order. Enjoy your evening.''

Christina tightened her grip on her menu and sat down. She was trying to enjoy herself. If she wasn't, it must be her own fault. She certainly couldn't blame her failure on her escort.

Kevin had shown up on time, in a slub silk jacket and a gold-tone SUV, both of which complemented his blond good looks. He held her coat. He opened her door. He turned on National Public Radio in the car and made polite conversation as they drove.

''Did I tell you how very lovely you look tonight?'' he asked now, leaning forward, his eyes warm and his voice earnest.

And she thought that was nice of him, the flattering

admiration in his eyes and the practiced sincerity in his voice, but they left her flat. No zings. Not a single tingle.

She made an effort to respond. "Thank you."

Jack's voice drawled derisively in her head. *You're female, breathing, not bad to look at.*

Go away, she thought at him.

But of course he wouldn't go away. He would be here any minute.

"I'll follow you in the truck," he'd informed her after Christina had refused to break her date.

She'd sneered. "You mean, you're not going to sit between us in the car?"

"Only if you move into the back seat."

Hot blood rose in her cheeks. "But if Kevin isn't a danger—"

"*Maybe* he isn't a danger." Jack cut her off. "It's damned unlikely he's been working underground for Tamir for twenty years on the off chance that one day they'd need some microbiologist in Montana to kidnap a princess. But not being a mole doesn't automatically mean he's qualified to protect you if the real bad guys show up."

Christina listened to Kevin order a bottle of Fayrene's best merlot and thought that surely a man ought to be judged for more than his ability to stop speeding bullets.

Like Jack did.

Her mind skittered off to his shattered shoulder, his shattered career, his voice, stretched tight over pain in the dark. Jack.

She remembered his hot, hard body pressing down on hers, the wild glory of his kiss, and her breasts got tight and her muscles got loose and warm. Zings and tingles, all the way.

For pity's sake. She bunched her heavy linen napkin in her lap. She really should not be sitting here across from

Kevin Atkins fantasizing about another man. She was a terrible date.

But then, she rationalized, she hadn't had much practice. Any practice. Perhaps she would improve? She listened to Kevin expounding on his latest government grant and sighed.

Or perhaps she should just fall on her salad fork and flop facefirst into her Roquefort dressing.

Kevin's voice changed pitch. "Isn't that your friend? The one visiting from out of town?"

Her heart picked up speed. Elaborately casual, she glanced toward the bar. And there he was, tall and lean and dangerous looking, his jaw scraped smooth, his hair combed back. Oh, yes. Jack. He wore pressed black jeans, a dark leather jacket and a forbidding expression. The hostess fluttered around him.

Christina fluttered, too. Inside, where no one could see.

"I believe so, yes," she said coolly.

"What's he doing here?"

She shrugged. "Having dinner, probably."

Kevin frowned. "Is he meeting someone?"

Yes. *Me.*

Guilt stirred. "I really have no idea. I don't keep tabs on what he does or who he sees."

Kevin's handsome, unhappy face cleared. "No, of course not. He's not really your type, is he? Our little hostess looks more his speed."

Christina risked another glance. The hostess was just seating Jack at a table in a nearby corner, where he had a good view of the room and their booth.

And of the hostess.

Christina's teeth snapped together. The pretty brunette was leaning across Jack's arm to open his menu, and he had a very, very good view of the hostess.

"Friend of the family, you said?" Kevin sounded indulgent.

She jerked her gaze back to her own table. "His father...works...for my father."

Kevin beamed. "You know, that's one of the things I've always admired about you, Christina. For a member of a moribund political system, you've always been astonishingly democratic."

He had her attention now. She straightened on her high-backed bench.

"'Moribund political system'?" she repeated carefully as the waiter, Roger, arrived with their steaks.

"Well...the monarchy." With a wave of his hand, Kevin dismissed more than a hundred years of continuous rule, her father's statesmanship and her people's heritage. "'Long live the king' is a bit outdated, isn't it?"

"That's remarkably insensitive of you, considering that the next king, my brother, is missing and presumed dead."

Kevin had the grace to flush. "Sorry. I just meant that as a system of government, the monarchy is increasingly irrelevant in today's world. After all, it's not like a king actually does anything. Not like the old days."

Christina tried counting to ten—she was a princess, after all—but it was no good. She still wanted to stab him with her horn-handled steak knife. "So, you consider me to be irrelevant."

"No, no. You're to be commended for leaving all that behind." When she only stared at him over her cooling and untouched steak, Kevin cleared his throat. "Not that your notoriety doesn't have its uses, of course."

She felt like Alice, stumbling through the looking glass. This evening wasn't going where she expected at all. "Excuse me?"

"It would certainly be regrettable if the department's

credibility were undercut by the wrong kind of attention. But there's no getting around the fact that you are in a unique position to publicize our work in San Diego next week."

Christina forced herself to release her death grip on her napkin. "Because of my research," she said stiffly. Surely he would agree with her? "Because I am speaking at the conference."

"Well," Kevin swallowed and reached for his wine-glass. "That, too, of course. I'm sure the program committee considered your publication record when they invited you."

"What else would they consider?"

He continued to smile at her while he stripped her of her hard-won identity. "Don't be naive, Dr. Sebastiani. Or should I say, Princess Christina? It's not often a biology symposium attracts a glamour spokeswoman."

The dining room faded into muffled, dull confusion at the edge of her awareness. She felt slightly sick. "I'm not going as a spokeswoman. I'm going as a scientist."

The assistant department chairman waggled his fork at her. "The important thing is, you're going. You'll be there. And so will the cameras. It's excellent public relations for everyone. Wear something pretty, and we might even get some funding out of it."

She narrowed her eyes in a look that would have made her father proud. "I am participating in a workshop. Not a photo opportunity."

"You should be grateful you're participating at all. Remember that, and give the organizers what they want. As a relatively junior colleague, it wouldn't be that difficult to replace you on the program."

Christina stuck out her jaw. "You would be amazed at how difficult I'm prepared to make things, Kevin."

"Now, Christina." He leaned forward and covered her hand with his. "You don't want to do anything to embarrass the department."

A male voice broke in roughly on their discussion. "I don't think she could do anything that would embarrass you, Atkins. You seem pretty shameless to me."

Christina looked up. "Jack!"

He loomed by their table, thumbs hitched in his pockets, his face dark. Christina drew her hand away, both mortified and relieved. How much had he heard?

"You done here?" he asked.

"I—"

Kevin spoke sharply. "Don't be foolish. You've barely touched your food."

She lifted her chin. "Yes, I believe I am all finished here."

Jack nodded once. "Let's go, then."

She stood. "Thank you for a very…enlightening evening, Kevin. Enjoy your dessert."

Jack escorted her from the dining room in silence. The parking lot was dark. The air was cold. The sky was pricked with stars.

Christina shivered. "Thank you for coming over."

He unlocked the truck and then handed her her keys. "You're welcome."

"Why *did* you come over?"

He walked around the hood and slid in beside her. "You looked upset."

"I was," she admitted. She slammed her door and adjusted her seat belt, but she couldn't seem to summon the energy to start the car.

Jack leaned against the passenger window. His shoulders blocked the night outside. "He make a pass?"

She laughed shakily. "No."

"Then what was that stuff about you embarrassing the department?"

"Nothing. It doesn't matter."

"Right. You're not the type to get upset over nothing," he observed.

She squeezed the steering wheel tighter, holding on to her control. "Thank you for that."

The outline of his shoulders moved in a shrug. "No problem."

She still didn't start the car. She could feel him watching. Waiting.

"What do you think of Montebello's political system?" she asked suddenly.

His surprise reached through the dark. "Is this a quiz?"

"Just answer, please."

"Hell, it doesn't matter what I think. What's important is how you feel about it. How the people who live there feel about it."

He was right, and yet... She wanted his support. Somehow over the past few days his opinion had started to matter to her. "Do you think the monarchy is moribund?"

"Dying, you mean?"

"Obsolete."

"No," he answered slowly. "I'm not a political analyst or anything like that, but—no. When the English pulled out, your family kept the island stable."

"That was over a hundred years ago."

"Yeah. But your father is still an active leader. He rallied the island against that Arab takeover. He was instrumental in allowing our forces to set up a base there. An obsolete ruler couldn't have done either of those things."

"My father is an extraordinary man. He would be a great leader even without being monarch."

"Maybe. But I'm a Navy SEAL. Was a Navy SEAL," Jack corrected himself, but this time there was no bitterness in his voice. "We understand pride. We believe in service. We appreciate tradition. Seems to me the monarchy is about pride and service and tradition."

"And photo opportunities," Christina said bitterly. She started the car. "And public relations."

"Isn't that service, too?"

She turned on her headlights and glared through the windshield. "You can't compare negotiating military treaties with playing glamour spokesperson for every opportunist who wants a royal card to draw media attention."

"You think? What did Atkins want tonight?"

She had thought he wanted a date. Her vanity was wounded. But more, her sense of herself as a contributing member of the scientific community had suffered a blow. She reversed out of her parking space. "He wants to use me. He suggested I use my—my notoriety to draw attention to the conference."

"Why?"

"Fund-raising."

"Yeah, well, you wouldn't want the cause of land reclamation to get more funding," Jack said, straight-faced. "You want me to go back and punch him out?"

Christina signaled her turn out of the lot onto the dark road, trying to sieve the frustration from her voice. "You don't understand. I worked too hard to establish my credentials in a male-dominated field to undercut them by playing part-time princess for the cameras. Don't you see?"

"I see you making this pretty damn complicated, making yourself out to be two different people. You are a scientist. You're also a princess. What are you committed to?"

No one spoke to her like that. "Excuse me?"

"Forget about who you are. What is your commitment? If it's getting plants to grow in mine areas, then you do whatever it takes to get the job done. You study. You put in the long hours in the lab. And if you have to, you make nice for the cameras to raise research money."

He was challenging *her* dedication? She was stung. The truck barreled around a corner and snarled up an incline.

"Don't talk to me about commitment. I've devoted the last ten years of my life to researching beneficial bacteria. What about you?"

"I was a SEAL, cupcake. You don't get more committed than that."

Her breath hissed. She might have rejected "your royal highness" in favor of "doctor." That didn't mean she had to take "cupcake" lying down.

"And what about now?" she demanded. "What is it that you're committed to now, Mr. Used-to-be-a-SEAL?"

"At the moment, I'm responsible for saving your ass."

"That's wonderful. *For the moment*. What about when this assignment is over?" She wasn't asking just because she was furious. She genuinely wanted to know.

"What the hell does it matter?"

"Well, because…" She did not understand his disregard of his future. Could not accept it. Sometimes she felt she had spent her entire life planning. "You should be thinking about your prospects."

"Why? As you so nicely pointed out, princess, my career is washed up. I don't have prospects anymore."

His harsh tone shook her. She slowed to take the next curve, uncertain in the darkness. "That's ridiculous. You can't define your life by your limitations."

"This from the princess-in-hiding?"

"Don't you dare judge my life."

"Then you butt out of mine."

Chapter 9

Jack paid the delivery boy in the car port, dropped the bag from the one-hour photo shop in on top of the groceries and started up the flagstone walk. He could feel the cold weight of a sirloin and a six-pack through the stiff brown bag. But the weight and the chill in his arms couldn't touch the atmosphere inside the house.

For the past thirty-six hours, Christina had wrapped herself in a blanket of work and wounded dignity that was tough to take and had to be even harder to pull off.

Jack shifted the groceries to unlock the front door. She managed it, though. Royally. Beautifully. With a cool, don't-touch-me grace and without once ever giving him the opportunity to accuse her of a lack of cooperation. Without once ever stooping to anything so common as sulking.

If he wasn't so ticked off, he would have given her a damned standing ovation.

She met him in the foyer with her defenses nailed to the

flagpole and her pride flying. "I didn't hear the bell ring. Who was that?"

He hefted the bag in his right arm. "Dinner. I caught the guy before he came up."

"Oh. Thank you. I should reimburse you."

He didn't want her money. Not for feeding her. Not for protecting her. Which raised a couple of interesting questions, like, what did he think he was going to live on? Or hope he could take in trade?

"I'll add it to my tab," he said gruffly.

"Of course." She cleared her throat. "I thought it might be the crew from Confidentially Yours."

"You hire an escort service?" he teased, hoping she would laugh. Or snap. Or bop him one.

He was disappointed. She just tilted that regal little chin and looked down her aristocratic nose at him. "A cleaning service. They come in on Mondays to do the house and yard and change the linens."

"Call them and cancel."

"No, I—"

"I don't want strangers in the house."

"These aren't strangers. I've used them for years. They're very exclusive."

"Uh-huh. How many exclusive cleaning services are there in the area, princess? Anybody who wanted access to your house could use them as cover."

"That's nonsense. The company has very low turnover. I know the people who clean my house."

"Maybe well enough to pick them out in a lineup. Do you even know their names?"

Her blue eyes clouded uncertainly. "Of course I do. There's Mary…"

"Uh-huh. Last name?"

She hesitated. "Smith, I think."

"Oh, great. That really narrows down our suspects if somebody decides to plant a bug on you. Or a bomb." He strode toward the kitchen, calling over his shoulder, "Call them and cancel. Now."

She followed him, protesting. At least she was speaking to him. "I actually prefer living in a clean house."

He dumped the grocery bag onto the counter. "Fine. Then I'll clean it. After I get dinner started."

"That's not what I was suggesting. It's not your job."

He had a sudden memory of her clear, bitter voice from that night in her tent. *I certainly wouldn't want you to do anything that's not in your contract.* Like take her in a sleeping bag. Or against the counter. Or on top of the kitchen table, her pale hair spilling over the edge while he pushed between her long, smooth thighs....

His blood surged. His stomach muscles contracted. Frustration—pure sexual frustration—roughened his voice. "Princess, I've polished brass and scrubbed latrines. I think I can handle your fancy vacuum cleaner."

"Wonderful. So can I."

He thwacked down a plastic meat tray, followed by a couple of baking potatoes. "Do you want to do it?" he challenged her.

"Yes. Why not?"

"You ever do it before?"

"I can certainly figure it out. I told you, I don't believe in defining myself by my limitations." Her eyes narrowed as she added sweetly, "Maybe I want the experience."

Oh, man. Oh, *yeah.*

Jack sucked in his breath. Easy, Flash. She was baiting him. And while he'd been trying for two days to get a rise from her, right now he didn't trust his own control. He wanted her out of the kitchen before he gave her an experience they'd both regret.

He waved a hand toward the utility closet, where he'd found the vacuum cleaner when he was rummaging for supplies. "Fine. Be my guest."

She raised her eyebrows. "Aren't you forgetting something?"

"What?"

She treated him to a small, cool smile. "Technically, you are my guest. I don't need your permission to clean my house."

Okay, so she had him there. He grinned and shook his head as she pivoted on her small, neat heel and sashayed to the closet. She looked really good in flat sneakers and tight jeans, like Grace Kelly slumming.

But he remembered her smooth and hot and under him, and it was all he could do not to go in after her, back her up against the broom and bucket, and do his damnedest to shatter that frosty reserve.

Her hands were shaking, actually shaking, as she plugged the vacuum cord into the outlet in the upstairs hall.

Christina frowned. She was not upset. She was a Sebastiani. She would not allow herself to be upset. She would not let one macho, underfoot, former Navy SEAL upset her. Why should it matter to her if he dismissed his tremendous potential? Why should it matter if he ignored her? As he kept pointing out with aggravating steadiness, this was a purely temporary arrangement for both of them.

Jack was simply doing his job, and she... She sighed. She didn't know what she was doing.

She straightened and studied the vacuum. So, all right, it was plugged in. And there was a switch thing on the handle marked Off, so if she slid it this way... The machine roared to life, and she smiled.

She had carried the vacuum upstairs, reluctant to experiment under Jack's knowledgeable, skeptical eyes. But there was nothing to it, really. All she had to do now was push it around. She gave it a nudge. It stayed stubbornly still, the handle locked in an upright position.

Not a problem. She was not going to be defeated by a common household appliance. Or intimidated by a common American sailor.

She thought of Jack's superbly disciplined body, his brazen good looks, his unquestioned competence, and sighed again. All right, maybe not so common.

But she was smart, and she was determined. Despite her lack of experience, she would figure both of them out.

She found a lever on the bottom of the machine and pressed it with her foot. The handle of the vacuum dropped back, hitting her thigh, and the vacuum moved forward. Christina pushed it up and down the hall, making nice neat lines in the plush, neutral carpet. It was oddly soothing. The vacuum's hum drowned out her busy thoughts and the sound of Jack bumping around in her kitchen.

When she thought she had the hang of it, she opened the door of his room.

He had only been there a few days, and already the room was marked by his presence, the bed made up with military precision, his few personal possessions marching in a line across the dresser. A comb, his keys, a folded bit of paper. The air even smelled like him, like shaving cream and man and leather and some faint chemical smell she couldn't identify. She felt an unfamiliar heat start low in her belly, and took a deep breath. She wanted to breathe him in, to take him in and hold him inside her.

Not a good thought.

Not a safe thought.

But irresistible.

What was she doing here? She stood in his room, her heart knocking a warning against her ribs, the vacuum beating against the carpet.

Oh, for pity's sake. She had a job to do, no less than he did. In two days, she was leaving for the microbiology conference in San Diego. And in the meantime, she was cleaning the man's room. Just as millions of other women all over the world swept and swabbed and dusted.

She switched off the vacuum and swiped at the already clear surfaces of the nightstand and bureau. No pictures, she noticed. He had mentioned a sister. Was there also a girlfriend? Or girlfriends? What did they say about sailors? A woman in every port?

She winced as her own words came back to her. *Don't you dare judge my life.*

Then you butt out of mine.

Yes. Hadn't she learned that was better? Safer. Privacy was her best protection. She could not afford to be curious about Jack Dalton. He didn't want her interest, anyway— not in his life, not in his pain, not in his hard, lean body. She could offer him nothing but courtesy.

And clean towels, she thought. The realization left her oddly dissatisfied.

She went into the hall and got a full set of fresh towels from the linen closet. She crossed his room, leaving tracks on the freshly vacuumed carpet, and opened the door of the guest bath.

A dim red light shone over the sink, and the faucet looked funny. She paused, surprised. The chemical smell was much stronger in here. What looked like half of an overhead projector was sitting on the counter, and a line was draped along the shower curtain rod and from there to the towel rack. Laundry? But...

She started when she saw her face swim in front of her,

a pale red oval in the dark. Her heart bumped. The mirror, she thought, feeling foolish. But no, the mirror was to her left, and the image was small, in front of her, swaying beside another and another and— She snapped on the overhead light, and, oh, God, they were all her, black-and-white pennants of her face, her body.

Photographs.

She gaped at them, feeling sick. Sandbagged. Jack had to have taken them. They were in his bathroom. He must have taken them. Developed them.

She'd *told* him she didn't like having her picture taken, and he'd said—he'd said... She struggled to remember.

I hate to break it to you, princess, but you're not the only scenic view around here.

She closed her eyes. But behind her closed lids, the images danced, mocking her.

Jack glanced toward the curving, honey-colored stairs. It sure was quiet up there. He hadn't heard the vacuum for a while. Was Princess Cinderella having trouble? *In* trouble?

He covered a steel bowl of sliced mushrooms and onions and took the steps two at a time.

The door to his room was open. No sound came from inside. He paused at the top of the stairs. "Christina?"

No answer.

He prowled inside, past the silent, upright vacuum standing sentinel on the carpet. "Everything okay?"

There. She stood framed in the doorway of his bathroom-turned-darkroom, her arms full of dark blue towels and her face set and pale.

Hell. Obviously, she'd discovered his setup. Just as obviously, she wasn't thrilled about it.

"What's up?" he asked casually.

Wrong approach. Her eyes iced over like the Arctic Sea. She turned that blank, cold gaze toward the open door behind her, and said, "Perhaps you should tell me."

He had the feeling explanations weren't going to do him much good. He'd planned on showing her the color shots first. When she saw how well they had turned out, how much they would add to her presentation, she wouldn't mind the rest. "Oh, the pictures. Yeah. I have more downstairs."

"More?" she asked faintly.

Why did she sound so appalled? "Extra shots. Slides for your workshop. I don't do my own color developing away from a lab."

She just stared at him.

"You're upset."

A faint color suffused her cheeks. She opened her mouth. Closed it. Twice. "Yes," she said finally, carefully. "I am upset."

He could see that. "I'm sorry." He wasn't used to apologizing, but her reaction clearly indicated something extraordinary was called for. "It's kind of second nature for me, shooting pictures. I figured as long as you didn't notice—"

"If you snuck them in, you mean?" It wasn't embarrassment staining her face, he realized. It was anger.

"If I stayed out of your way," he corrected her doggedly, "it wouldn't matter. Cameras make some people self-conscious. I thought if I was discreet—"

"You didn't think. You knew I didn't want you to take my picture. I told you so."

Her tone—and his own sense of guilt—flayed him. He struck back defensively. "Look, it's not as if you've never had your picture taken before. These aren't even topless."

She recoiled as if he'd slapped her. "That was completely different."

"Yeah, that was public."

She hugged the pile of towels to her chest. "And do you think that I knew that? Do you honestly suppose I stripped off my top and marched into cold water and shouted, 'Please, take my picture—oh, and send copies to every paper in the world'?"

Her reaction confused him. "No, but..." Her face was closed, her arms crossed against him. Frustrated, he tried again. "People in your position have to expect a certain level of interest from the press. If some paparazzi character—"

"The picture you refer to was not taken by a member of the paparazzi." Her voice could have cut glass.

Ah, hell.

"Peeping Tom?" he asked, not really believing it.

"No."

His gut tightened. "Lover?"

She looked away. "Someone I knew."

Her downcast eyes said it: someone she trusted. The way, presumably, she was supposed to be able to trust Jack. Damn.

"Who?" he asked harshly.

"Ryan Cunningham, twenty-one, a film student at UCLA," she said in her cool, precise way, as if reducing the whole ugly mess to newspaper statistics made it more distant. More bearable. "He wanted to produce, but he was a better actor. Or perhaps I was simply gullible. And he was handsome, in a California sort of way."

Jack conjured up a blond, long-haired surfer dude, all tan and teeth. He bristled. "Did he force you to pose? Pressure you?"

"Oh, no. It was much more insidious than that. Ryan

respected me too much ever to take advantage.'' Her thin smile twisted. "I should have seen through that right away. I never dreamed…"

"That he'd take your picture," Jack finished grimly. He'd really screwed up here. Without meaning to, maybe, but he'd definitely screwed up.

"That he would sell my picture," Christina corrected.

Jack frowned. "Why did he? If you two were close—"

"He had nothing else left to gain from the relationship. We broke up," she explained. "I broke up with him."

Jack wouldn't make the mistake of judging her again. She'd probably been just a kid at the time, in a country and a situation she wasn't prepared for. "He should have seen it coming. He was a commoner, right? An American? Your family wouldn't have liked that."

"I liked it," she said, dumbfounding him. "I wanted a common American." Her smile flickered again like a knife blade in the dark. "Well, I was very young. And rebellious. And eager for what I imagined was a normal life."

He could see that. He could picture her, an independent twenty-one-year-old with stars in her eyes and dreams in her heart for an ordinary life with Mr. All-American. "So, what was the problem?"

She put the towels down on the bed and smoothed her palms over them. "Ryan was a whole lot more interested in me staying a princess than I was."

Her voice was flat. Depressed. Jack couldn't stand that, so he tried to cheer her up. "What, he wanted you to wear your tiara to bed?"

"He didn't want me in bed at all. He said he wanted me to have the fairy tale wedding at the palace with the bride all in white."

"What a loser."

"Thank you," she said politely. "I needed to be reminded of my lousy taste in men."

Obviously, the cheering up stuff wasn't working. "So, he went public with the pictures, and you broke with him."

"No, I broke with him, and then he sold the pictures. If he wasn't going to get the publicity perks that went with dating me, at least he could use me to finance his first film."

Son of a bitch. "He was a user. Forget it. Forget him."

Her chin lifted. "And the pictures draped all over your darkroom? Am I just supposed to forget those, too?"

He wished she would. He understood her suspicion. But he was surprised how much it stung. "No. You don't have any reason to trust me."

"I did trust you." Past tense, he noted, wincing. Her eyes were angry and bright. "It's my own judgment I don't trust. My family—they stood behind me after that awful picture came out, but I know I disappointed them."

"You couldn't have known your boyfriend would go public with those shots."

Her lips pressed together. "No. But I knew he took them. I went with him into the mountains, only for the day…. But I let my guard down."

And she would not forgive herself for that, Jack thought. Or him, either.

"So, are you worried now I'm going to use you to bankroll my retirement?"

Her blue eyes searched his. "No," she said finally. "You told me yourself you're not planning for the future. Maybe you are protecting me for the money. But I don't think you're financing your next career move selling my picture to the tabloids."

He was almost glad she considered him too shiftless to take advantage of her. That was pathetic.

"What I would like to know," she said clearly, "is why you would take my picture at all."

"You're kidding, right?"

"No." She frowned. "It's not some sort of report you're doing for my father, is it?"

"Hell, no."

"Then, why?" she insisted.

She couldn't be that clueless. If her intention was to embarrass him, she was succeeding. He felt like a twelve-year-old dork caught hanging around the popular girl's locker at school.

"Maybe I just wanted them to decorate my bathroom," he said.

"Like pinup posters?" She shook her head. "Try again, sailor."

Beneath the chilly, in-control tone, he heard an uncertainty that tore him up. She really didn't have a clue, he realized. She had no idea how compelling she was to him as a photographer. And as a man.

"Why not? You're beautiful enough."

She rolled her eyes. "I'm blond. That, and being a Sebastiani, is enough to get me media attention. It doesn't explain yours."

Suddenly it was important that she see herself as he saw her. Not just to dig himself out of a hole. But because— well, because he was beginning to like her. A lot, even though she could be prickly and prissy. She was special. He figured she ought to know that.

There were risks, of course. Like any sleeping princess, Christina was well-guarded by thorns. An awkward attempt to reach her could provoke her into laughter.

Or shock her into flight.

But if he could only make her see how incredible she

was, maybe he could repair the careless wound left by her long-ago boyfriend.

Jack smiled grimly. Assuming, of course, he could touch her without losing his own hard-held control.

He took a step toward her, pleased when she didn't retreat. "You're overestimating me, sweetheart. I'm as susceptible as the next guy to a gorgeous blonde." He reached out to rub a strand of her hair between his fingers. She jolted and then stood, trapped by his hold on her hair. "And the first time I pulled out my camera, don't think I didn't notice that you've got nice legs. And breasts. You've got great breasts."

Color swept into her face. He watched it, watched her tongue come out to moisten her lips. "But that's not me. I'm a biologist. The other—that's just packaging."

He held her gaze steadily. "But it's the whole package that I like. The blond microbial ecologist princess." He let himself smile, inviting her to share the absurdity of it, and the delight. "There are magazines that would go nuts for a spread like that."

"You make me sound like someone's sweaty fantasy," she said crossly.

"Yeah," he admitted. "Mine."

She shivered. "No. That's not me."

"It could be." He moved in on her, feeling the heat in his body. Seeing the heat in her eyes. "Let me show you."

Chapter 10

Jack's hand slid from Christina's hair to her shoulder. His thumb rubbed her lightly, making her breath catch. Her brain slowed. Her blood thickened.

His face was very close. She could see each eyelash and the hard dip of his upper lip and the darkness of his eyes.

He pulled on her shoulder, turning her toward the bathroom. "Come see my pictures."

She took two slow steps toward the narrow doorway, struggling for balance in a rising tide that sucked at her feet and her resolution. "Is that anything like 'Come look at my etchings'?"

She felt his amusement as a puff of warm air on the back of her neck. "If I say yes, will you bolt?"

"I don't know," she answered honestly. "Am I going to be embarrassed?"

"No dirty pictures," he promised. "Just some photographs of you."

"That's what I'm afraid of," she muttered. But she

straightened her shoulders against his guiding hand and marched ahead of him into his jerry-rigged darkroom.

Drying prints still swagged the walls and shower curtain. She flinched from the shadowed images of her own face, the angles of her own body.

"Tell me what you see," Jack said low in her ear.

She swallowed. "You want me to compliment you on your technique now?"

"Not until I do something you like." *Oh, heavens,* she thought. "Concentrate on the subject," he said.

Her gaze swept the sagging row. She wasn't in every photograph. She admired a study of leaves, a silhouette of trees, a swirl of dark water. She felt a pang over a shot of Eric Hunter's profile as he watched the other boys on the bank, his glum face in stark contrast to the braced casualness of his pose. Pain and exclusion were subjects Jack Dalton understood.

But there were still way too many pictures of her. Her face, frowning over a collection tray, laughing as she listened to a student. Her body, crouched or stretched or in fluid motion. She felt as exposed as if it were her underwear hanging there on the line.

"What do you see?" Jack asked again.

"I see a great many pictures you had no right to take."

He shook his head like a disappointed teacher. "You're not looking closely enough." He moved up behind her again, so that she felt him warm and solid at her back. "Look at you. Look at yourself the way I see you."

Her pulse kicked. "I am completely indifferent to how you see me," she lied.

"You don't sound indifferent," he said, his voice ruffling her senses. "You sound...excited."

She looked nervously over her shoulder. He watched her, his eyes dark and steady on her face, and all right, yes, he was so big and close and hot, of course she was excited. Only what good did it do her? Any minute now he would remember what she was and where they were and throw her out.

"I'll try to control myself. I remember you don't like me to get excited."

"What the hell kind of crack is that?"

"Oh, that's right," she said, nodding sagely. "It was my lack of experience you objected to."

"Experience isn't the issue here. You're sex over ice, cupcake," he said, and this time she didn't even think to take offense. "A guy could get drunk on that face of yours. Look at your face." He reached over her shoulder to stab a finger at one of the pictures hanging on the line.

He must have taken the shot in the lab, she thought. Her hair was pulled back. Her goggles dangled around her neck. She looked untidy and unsmiling.

"I've seen my face," she said uncomfortably. "I see it every day."

"You don't see anything."

Her heart was beating fast. Too fast. She jerked her chin up. "I'm a scientist. I make detailed observations all the time. And any woman who puts on makeup is familiar with her own face."

He shook his head, so close she could imagine the brush of his jaw against her cheek. "You take that face apart, feature by feature, it's nice enough. But it's the way it's put together that makes it so damn beautiful. All the collisions. All the contradictions."

His thumb reached to trace a curve in the photograph. She shivered as if he touched her skin. "Here's this jawline, real delicate, and then it smacks into this stubborn chin." He tapped it with his finger. "Contradiction, see?

Like the really sharp eyes and then the mouth, kind of pouty. Sexy.''

The pad of his finger ran over the photographed shape of her lips. She swallowed hard. He traced another line on the paper, his voice warm and low beside her ear. ''Or the snooty nose, and then this little pleat above your eyebrows. I didn't get it all. I could shoot a thousand frames and still not get all of you on film.''

She was trembling. ''Why would you even want to?''

He turned her in his arms. His eyes, dark and hot, devoured her.

''The American Indians used to believe a picture could capture your soul,'' he whispered. ''Maybe I want your soul, Christina.''

Her breath deserted her. Her heart pounded. And then his head lowered and his mouth took hers with a lazy, casual assurance that offended her pride and thrilled her body.

He was big and hot and close. Overwhelming. He smelled like aftershave and healthy male, and his chest felt solid and warm along the front of her, along her breasts and belly, and his shirt felt rough and in the way.

She wanted him closer. She opened her mouth, and he thrust inside, moving with a rhythm she vaguely recognized and welcomed. His jaw rasped her face. His tongue ravaged her mouth. He took a step, backing her into the counter, and the cold marble hit her hips and jolted her forward into his heat. His belt buckle dug into her ribs. His arousal prodded her stomach.

It felt wonderful. He felt wonderful, thick and exciting and male.

And even though she knew it was wrong, even though she suspected he would drop her cold the minute he recalled who she was and why they shouldn't be doing this, she wrapped her arms tight around him and sank into his kiss.

Her hands clutched at the strong column of his neck, at the short strands of his hair. He growled encouragement, moving one broad hand down her back, shifting her against the marble so that her thighs moved apart and he could make a place for himself between them. The fit, body-to-body, his hardness to her softness, made her gasp.

He fisted a hand in her hair and pulled her head back so that he could stare into her face. His was hard, almost primitive. Slowly, deliberately, he rubbed himself against her, and she made a choked sound in her throat and arched into him.

He held her back. "How far do you want this to go?" he asked harshly.

She was beyond thinking. She was all wanting. "I don't know. I don't know what to do, what you want—"

"What do you want?" he interrupted her.

The heat of her need evaporated her pride. "This," she said. "More."

"I'll give you more," he promised, and his mouth descended again with shattering force.

Deep, delicious, mindless kisses later, his hand came up to cup her breast. She felt him measure the weight of it, and the softness, before he pushed open the neckline of her shirt and slipped his hand inside. He palmed it, his hand warm and a little rough through the silken barrier of her bra, before he curled his fingers and plucked at the tight nipple. She sucked in a breath. He did, too. The sound of his excitement fed hers, made it leap and twist inside her like water escaping from a mountain cleft.

He pulled down the cup of her bra, the delicate lace rasping her more delicate flesh, freeing her to his untrammeled touch. To his hot, hungry eyes.

She blushed all the way from her belly button to her hairline, and he smiled with primal satisfaction.

"Beautiful," he said, and bent to take her nipple in his mouth.

His mouth was wet and warm and seeking on her breast. His hands were rough and urgent. He supported her with one strong arm behind her back while he feasted on her soft, damp flesh.

Sensation spiraled inside her. She had never felt like this. Despite anything she'd ever read in magazines or romance novels, she hadn't really believed anyone could feel like this. She quivered as he worked his way slowly up her torso, to the tender crease between her neck and shoulder, to the sensitive place behind her ear. He was breathing heavily. So was she.

"Nice. We'll finish this inside," he said.

That sounded dangerous.

It sounded…promising, she decided, and did not protest as he half dragged, half carried her through the doorway into his bedroom.

She had a moment's unease when he bumped the back of her knees against the box spring and paused to peel the shirt off her shoulders. Her hands fluttered to cover her breasts, but he only caught them in an easy clasp and held them away. His eyes narrowed as he studied her body.

"So damn beautiful," he said, and the hoarseness in his voice stripped away her inhibitions as easily as his hands divested her of slacks and socks.

He lowered her onto the king-size bed, the mattress dipping to take their weight, the cool spread sliding under her, her hands gripping his shoulders.

"Shouldn't you…?" She tugged at the fabric under her fingers, but he didn't stop to take off his own clothes.

He came down on her, heavy and hot, using his hands

to make her shake and shiver and his knee to push her thighs apart and his mouth to make her moan. Frustrated, she tried to yank his T-shirt free from the waistband of his jeans.

But then his wide, callused palm glided over the curve of her stomach and under the elastic of her panties, and his fingers touched her, there, between her legs, and she forgot his shirt and all the other barriers between them as he stroked her. He touched her in ways and places no one ever had touched her before. Her hands clenched, and her breath came short and fast, and she thought she might die of the pleasure and the pressure and the power of his touch.

"You're wet," he said, and that was really embarrassing, except he sounded so pleased and it felt so good.

She pushed her hips up, into his hand, and he made a sound of dark pleasure and kissed her again, his mouth demanding. Everything he asked of her she gave, twisting under him on the bed, her naked thighs rubbing against rock-solid muscle and smooth denim.

Something jangled at the edges of her mind. A warning? The phone.

The telephone was ringing.

She opened her eyes. Jack's face, hard and intent, hovered over hers. His eyes were dark and hot.

She licked her lips. "The phone...?"

"Forget the phone."

He kissed her again, and the pulsing of the phone was drowned out by the pounding of her heart, by the rush of sensation. He carried her through the flood, steering her with his wide, clever hands, and everything went dark behind her eyelids and inside her, a warm, breathing, shuddering darkness, and he nipped her shoulder as his hands moved, as his fingers moved, and she cried out and fell into the dark.

Jack felt the surge take her, felt her muscles tense and quiver as she was swept away. His own body throbbed with tension, ached with the control he'd imposed on it. His left arm trembled. His face and back were damp with sweat.

But he felt good. No, he felt great. Unless he knew a whole lot less about women than he thought he did, he'd just given Christina of Montebello her first male-induced climax.

He grinned with fierce satisfaction and snatched up the shrilling phone before it could call her back from her floating state. "Hello?"

"Jesus, Jack," his old man said in his ear. "If this is how long it takes you to answer the phone, you really are falling down on the job."

Christina clutched her blouse to her breasts. "What did you tell him?"

Jack sat on the edge of the mattress. He bent, presenting her with a view of his long, lean, muscled back, and scooped one of her socks from the floor. He tossed it to her. "I told him I would call him back. Get dressed."

She caught the sock one-handed. She was reluctant to drop the blouse. Even after all the wonderful, wicked, delicious things Jack had done to her breasts. Even after he'd touched, licked and sucked them. She felt shy in her own body, aware of it in ways she'd never considered before. She blushed.

"Did you tell him about us?"

"God, no."

Well. That was a relief. Wasn't it? Christina sat quietly, watching Jack tie his shoes. He'd taken off his shoes, at least. Otherwise he was completely dressed. And she was nearly naked.

"Why not?" she asked.

He looked at her over his shoulder. "Did you want him to know?"

She hugged the blouse a little tighter under her chin. "Of course not."

"Of course not," Jack drawled. He sounded bitter.

Christina dragged her lower lip back from a pout. What was his problem? He wasn't the one getting the back-to-business treatment after having his guard stripped and his composure shattered and his universe tilted on its axis by sex.

And then she realized. His universe hadn't tilted at all. Everything he'd done, he'd done to her and for her. She might be inexperienced, but she knew he had not found the satisfaction he'd brought her.

No wonder he was cranky.

She cleared her throat. "I'm sorry we didn't—you didn't…" He gave her an incredulous look over his shoulder. She shifted her legs under her, her blush and her discomfort growing. "Well, anyway, I'm sorry."

"Don't worry about it," he said.

She ought to be grateful. But she didn't like having him dismiss her concerns so lightly. She didn't like having him dismiss *her* so lightly.

"I think we should talk," she said.

He winced. "Look, I've got to call the old man. Let's talk later."

"How much later?"

He stood. "*Later* later. Christina, I've got a job to do."

Okay, not only hadn't his axis tilted, his world wasn't even rocked. Something that had been cataclysmic for her had barely registered on his Richter scale.

She lifted her chin. "Yes, and you always get the job done, don't you?"

He frowned. "What are you upset about? You got what you wanted."

"You didn't."

"I told you not to worry about it. All part of the service, all right?"

She nodded to cover her anger. "Like making dinner."

"What?"

She wriggled across the bedspread, trying to reach the edge of the mattress without losing hold of her shirt or her dignity. "'All part of the service.' Making dinner. Making love. Keep the princess happy."

He said, through his teeth, "The only thing I'm hired to do is keep you safe."

But he did not say their interlude on his bed meant anything to him.

He did not deny that he'd made love to her out of pity, after she'd blurted out her sorry little story of undergraduate love betrayed.

He did not say he wanted to do it again.

She straightened her shoulders. "So, what is dinner? Reward for my cooperation?"

He ran a hand through his hair in exasperation. "Look, we're living together. It only makes sense to share meals."

"And sex," she said coolly. She absolutely was not going to cry. "Obviously, it's only sensible to share that, too."

His blue eyes baffled, he stared at her, a satisfying picture of frustrated, angry male. "Sex isn't sensible, cupcake. Nothing about you and me is sensible."

He reached down and caught a strand of her hair between his thumb and forefinger. She sat still, barely breathing, as his hand glided down, tugging gently at her scalp, brushing lightly against her jaw.

"The hell of it is," he said huskily, "that when I'm

with you, I'm beginning not to care whether we make sense or not.''

"Okay, run that by me one more time," Jack said, adjusting the phone receiver under his ear.

Christina sat at the kitchen table, ignoring the papers spread out in front of her, watching him with distant blue eyes.

"The king refused the meeting." Jonathan Dalton sounded weary. "I thought we had something when Sheik Ahmed swore to take no action to jeopardize the princesses. But he wouldn't guarantee their safety, so Marcus canceled the meeting."

"The sheik still insists he's not responsible?"

"Not for the bombings and not for the kidnap attempt on Julia," Jonathan said. "But he's making land grab noises now, claiming Julia's child as his heir."

"How is my sister?" Christina asked, surprising him.

"How's Julia?" Jack repeated to his father.

"Three months pregnant," Jonathan answered grimly. "How should she be?"

Jack covered the mouthpiece with his palm. "She's okay. I think the pregnancy's causing some tension at home."

Christina nodded, her lips pressed together in concern.

Jack shifted his hand. "What about the threat to Christina?"

"Kamal claims he doesn't know anything about that."

"But the note—you've got lab results?"

"That tell us nothing. No identifying characteristics. No fingerprints. The paper stock was mass produced in the United States, the letter was mailed in Los Angeles."

"Christina did her undergrad at UCLA," Jack said slowly.

"There could be a connection," his father acknowledged.

"Get me a background on a Ryan Cunningham, would you? He was a film student when Christina was there."

Christina sat up. "No! I—"

"Do you have any reason to think he's involved?" Jonathan asked.

"Not really," Jack said, steadily holding Christina's glare. "But he did a number on her six years ago. I want to eliminate him as a suspect. And if you want to sic the IRS on him while you're at it, I'd be fine with that, too."

"I'll see what I can do," Jonathan promised dryly.

"Good. Anything else for me? Any other leads?"

"Nothing."

"I don't like it," Jack said. "I want to know who and what I'm supposed to be protecting her from. Why isn't the FBI in on this? Or the CTC?"

"Believe me, Jack, our government isn't ignoring the problem. The Counterterrorist Center has promised to inform us of any intelligence linking known terrorist groups to threats against the royal family. But until we can establish a connection, they are treating the letter to Christina as the work of an isolated nut case."

A kook. Christina had said the same.

"And what am I supposed to do in the meantime?" Jack asked.

"Watch out for her," Jonathan ordered. "And keep her away from California."

Hell. Jack said goodbye and hung up the phone. That might be easier said than done.

Christina sat with her laptop open and her presentation spread out around her. He didn't know what was in all those charts and notes, but they sure kept her busy. He

knew—because he'd kept an eye on her and the clock—
that she hadn't knocked off work until after one last night.

He admired her discipline. Once upon a time, he'd had
that kind of dedication, too. But it had been months since
anything had mattered that much. Nothing kept him awake
anymore. Except pain.

And her.

The thought scared him. She terrified him.

I think we should talk.

He had never in his life had a conversation with a
woman that began with those words that didn't end in
disaster. She would want things—assurances, commitment,
a future—that he couldn't give her.

Or she wouldn't want anything from him at all, and that
might be even worse.

"What now?" Christina asked quietly.

He grimaced. She was thinking long-term again. And he
had no long-term solutions, not for the danger that men-
aced her, not for the feelings that threatened to engulf him.

"We wait," he said. "And try to keep you safe."

"What about the note?"

"They don't know who sent it yet." They might never
know. There were limits to what even his father could do.
"I hoped maybe Kamal and the king would have come to
an agreement by now. But that's not happening."

Her gaze met his, warm and confident. "I can live with
it."

Possibility quickened his heart rate. Did she mean she
could live with him? But her next words squelched that
hope.

"One thing researchers learn to have is patience," she
said.

"Patience is good. But I was hoping for some kind of
progress. 'Wait and stay safe' isn't big with the Teams."

She raised those pretty eyebrows. "A real man of action," she said dryly.

She was teasing him. It felt good.

He grinned foolishly back. "I'll give you action."

She turned pink and looked down at her computer keyboard. "I believe you already did. I also don't think that's enough to keep you occupied for long."

"Cupcake, I was barely getting started."

But she refused to be diverted. "What will you do when you leave here, Jack?"

Uh-oh. The million dollar question. "Join the circus?" he suggested flippantly.

She gave him her bacteria-under-the-microscope look.

He shrugged. "I don't know. Anybody who makes it as a SEAL—why would he quit and do something else? Some guys go from the Teams into law enforcement or security. I knew one who became an Emergency Medical Technician. You do good. You get the thrill. But there can't be a lot of departments out there eager to take on an adrenaline junkie who can't lift one arm over his head."

"You could teach. Or go into administration."

"Ride a desk for the rest of my life?" He shook his head. "That's why I left the navy. I need to do more than that."

"You sound like Uncle Jonathan," she observed.

"The hell I do. My old man does what he does for the money."

"You do him an injustice. He is a good and loyal friend of my father's."

"Sure he is. Your daddy is paying him."

Her chin lifted. "And is that why you trouble yourself with me? Because your father is paying you?"

He scowled at her. "I don't want you to get hurt."

"Thank you very much. What does that have to do with anything?"

"I don't want you to see me as anything other than what I am. Just because I can scratch your itch doesn't make me some kind of hero."

She went rigid. But her voice was cool and perfectly composed. "Thank you," she said again. "That's very clear. If, in the future, I have any inclination to ascribe heroic attributes to you, I have only to remember that remark and I'm sure the feeling will go away."

Chapter 11

"Christina?" Julia Sebastiani sounded slightly stunned. Christina couldn't blame her. "I almost didn't believe it when Valerie said it was you on the line." She hesitated, then said weakly, "Isn't it very late where you are?"

"Eleven," Christina said. She gripped the receiver tighter. Now what? "I just, um…" She took a deep breath. "How are you?"

The phone line crackled. "If you're asking, I guess you know," her sister said at last, stiffly.

Christina winced. And then remembered what Jack had said: *When I was wounded…my kid sister called every day. And I was never so damn glad to hear from anybody in my life.*

"Yes," she said. "I—I heard."

"I suppose Mother phoned you?"

"She said you were doing well."

"Did she?" Julia gave a half laugh. "I guess she would, wouldn't she?"

Probably. The queen was a firm believer in putting a good face on things.

"So, are you? Well?" Christina asked.

"From a health point of view, which is Mother's pre-occupation at the moment, yes, I'm fine. It seems I'm getting over the morning sickness at last."

Oh, dear. It was hard to imagine her proud, lovely sister retching into a toilet.

"Is it very bad?" Christina asked sympathetically.

"The morning sickness? It's a bit like life at the palace," Julia said dryly. "You get used to it. And unlike life at the palace, sooner or later it does come to an—"

"No," Christina interrupted, feeling foolish. "I meant everything. Do you have everything you need?"

Ridiculous question. Julia had her own suite in the palace and her own staff: a personal maid, a chauffeur, business and social secretaries, cleaners and waiters, all trained to anticipate and fulfill her every need. She had complete service and a total lack of privacy.

Christina had run from both.

"Do I have everything I need?" Julia paused again. "Sure. Mother even has me taking vitamins."

Christina sighed in defeat. Why would Julia want to confide in her? But some strain in her sister's voice made her persist. "How is Mother taking it otherwise?"

"Oh." There was a long pause. A shaky breath. "She's being very understanding."

Ouch. The queen had been understanding six years ago, too, when Christina's breasts had flashed from newsstands worldwide. Gwendolyn's love for her children was unquestionable. But it made the burden of disappointing her even harder to bear.

"I hate letting her down like this," Julia said, in echo of Christina's thought.

"Tiss, are you all right?" Christina asked, unconsciously reverting to her sister's childhood nickname.

She sniffed. "Oh, God, Squidge, I've made such a mess of everything."

She was crying, Christina realized. Suddenly, silently crying. And her sister's hurt and the old nickname called up the childhood ghosts of two little girls in a palace. *Squidge, look, a kitten, let's take it home to Mama! Come on, Squidge, we're going to the beach. Squidge, let's put honey in the ambassador's hat.*

"Julia...I'm sure you haven't done anything wrong."

A choked laugh quavered over the line. "Wouldn't you call it wrong to sleep with our father's worst enemy's oldest son and heir? And now—oh, Squidge, everything's so awful."

"Oh, Julia..." It did sound awful, put like that. "How is Papa taking all this?"

"Papa..." There was a wealth of pain in the two syllables. "Oh, Papa is—he's stomping around being very His Majesty. A lot worse than that time we poured honey in the British ambassador's hat."

Christina could imagine.

"So, are you calling to tell me how my indiscretions have messed up your life, too?" Julia didn't sound offended, exactly. More like resigned.

Christina cleared her throat. "Actually, I called to ask advice."

That surprised another half-tearful laugh from her sister. "You're joking."

Not joking. Desperate. "No."

"You haven't asked for my advice in fifteen years, and you wait until I'm pregnant from a one-night stand to do so?"

"A one-night stand? Wow. Really?"

"Not exactly," Julia muttered. "I don't want to talk about it. I've had enough of trying to explain the inexplicable."

"All right," Christina said. "Don't explain. Just help me."

"Help you how? You always just do what you want."

Christina blinked. "I do not."

"Yes. You do. You always got out of things when we were children. I had to do the posing for the photographers. You were always 'away' or 'too shy.' And when Papa told you not to apply to school in the States, you did it anyway. And then when you got that scholarship to UCLA, you said you couldn't pass that up. And you got away with it."

"Because it's all I'm good at," Christina protested. "It's all that I wanted."

"Nice to be able to get what you want because you're brilliant and 'contributing something of value to the world,'" Julia said bleakly.

"Well." Christina regrouped. "I wasn't contributing anything at home. You make a much better princess than I do."

"I hardly had a choice, did I?"

This was a new view of her dutiful sister. "Did you want one?" Christina asked cautiously.

"I—oh, Squidge, what does it matter? It's water under the bridge. The point is, you took a stand years ago. And if I had had the courage to do the same, my life wouldn't be such a rotten mess now."

"It didn't feel courageous," Christina confessed. "It felt like running away. You were the perfect bride preparing for the wedding of the decade, and I was appearing topless on the cover of every trashy tabloid in the world."

"All I did was delay the headlines by five years." Julia's voice was flat. "I should have done what you did. Faced the scandal of breaking my engagement and gone after what I wanted."

"But...I thought you wanted to marry Luigi," Christina said.

"*Papa* wanted me to marry Luigi. I was having second thoughts. But then your film student published those awful pictures, and Papa swore another scandal would only make things worse." The line hummed. "And I have to say that seeing what you were going through made it much easier for him to persuade me. Luigi never wanted me, but he would have put me through hell in the tabloids if I dared break our engagement."

Christina thought of Ryan, who'd only wanted her for the publicity marriage would bring him, and Jack, who only wanted...well, who knew what Jack wanted? Not her. Not enough. Her voice sharpened in sympathy. "Luigi di Vitale Ferrelli was a self-absorbed bastard."

Julia laughed. "More than you will ever know," she said frankly, sounding warmer and more relaxed, more like a sister, than she had in a long time. "But compared to Rashid, he was an amateur."

"Julia, if there's anything I can do—"

"I wish I could come for a visit," Julia said wistfully. "I'd like to be closer to you. And to Lucas."

"Lucas is seven hundred miles away." And presumed dead, Christina thought but did not say. Her sister had enough troubling her without that reminder. "But I'm here if you need me, Tiss. And you'd love Montana. Think Colorado with fewer tourists."

Julia sighed. "It sounds perfect. Peaceful and uncomplicated."

"Actually," Christina said carefully, "Montana is a lot more complicated than it used to be."

Her palm grew sweaty on the receiver. It had been years since she'd whispered her dreams and disappointments to her big sister. They'd never giggled over crushes or shared stories after a big date.

"How so?" Julia asked.

"Even Montana has men," Christina said.

"Ah." Her sister's voice was affectionate. Teasing. "Not tidy like little bacteria, men. And which of Montana's stalwarts has confused your logical thinking to the point that you're asking for my advice?"

"His name is Jack Dalton. He's my—" Oh dear, it sounded so cliché. "—my bodyguard."

"Goodness." Silence crackled over the line. "Is this the man Papa insisted on hiring to protect you from Sheik Ahmed's potential kidnappers?"

"That's him."

Julia laughed with delight. "And you're sleeping with him? Sleeping with your bodyguard! Oh, Christina! I always thought you were—"

"I still am," Christina said. *Technically.* She had a sudden, molten memory of Jack's mouth, Jack's hands, and flushed hot. "I'm not sleeping with him yet. That's why I called you. For advice."

"Birth control," her sister said instantly.

Christina thought of Jack, hard and lean and fully dressed, pressing her into the mattress. "But we haven't—"

"It only takes one time," Julia warned. "I'm proof of that. You should buy birth control. If you got pregnant, too, Papa would have—I don't know—apoplexy or something."

Christina felt dizzy. Her dutiful sister was practically urging her to go for it. "All right."

"I must say, when you decide to break out, you certainly do it in style,'' Julia said admiringly. ''Your body-guard! That's rich.''

Christina winced. ''This isn't some sort of delayed ad-olescent-rebellion thing. I don't think. Actually, his father knows our father.''

''His father? Who—?''

''Jonathan Dalton.''

''Uncle Jonathan? Oh, I love him. He taught me to play chess. And this is his son?''

''His only son.''

''Papa will be pleased.''

''I, um, wasn't really planning on mentioning this to Papa.''

''No,'' Julia agreed instantly. ''Much better not. Well, if you've called for my blessing, little sister, I'd say follow your heart. And may you have better luck than I have. Do you love him?''

Did she? How could she judge? He was so different from any man she had ever encountered. No self-important academic in tweed and twill, no smooth palace attaché in a sleek Italian suit, no jaded playboy in six-hundred-dollar ski goggles had prepared her for former Navy SEAL Jack Dalton.

He was blunt and rough and competent. He took things as they were. He took her as she was. And when he touched her…

Don't see me as anything other than what I am. Just because I can scratch your itch doesn't make me some kind of hero.

''At the moment, I'd like to kill him,'' Christina said.

Julia laughed. ''Sounds like true love to me.''

True love?

''Oh, no,'' Christina said. Her sister was out of her mind. Stress could do that to a person. Or hormones. Or—

"But you do want to sleep with him," Julia persisted.

She swallowed hard. Possibly. And possibly she was the one who was crazy. "I haven't decided."

"Well, heaven help him if you ever make up your mind," her sister said. She sounded almost cheerful. "Maybe I should phone to warn him. Because when you do decide that you want something, Squidge, nothing and no one stands in your way."

Jack got off the phone and went in search of Christina. He found her in the greenhouse off the side of the garage, humming, her blond head bent over some ugly plant. Regret stabbed him. She was going to hate hearing this. He hated being the one to tell her.

In fact, the only upside to the situation was that she'd hate it so much that she'd go back to her princess in the tower routine, and maybe then he could remember he wasn't the white knight she deserved. Maybe then he could forget the way she felt arching into him, round and hot, the way she looked like heaven and smelled like sin.

She turned the plant on its side and eased it from the pot, her long-fingered, pretty hands sifting delicately through the dirt. He drew in a sharp breath.

Yeah, maybe. And maybe not.

"You know, sometimes you've got to accept that you can't have everything you want," he said.

Christina started, scattering dirt to the tile floor. Wild color bloomed in her face. "I—I beg your pardon?"

She was *really* going to hate this, Jack thought morosely.

"I just got off the phone with the general manager of the Harborside Hotel in San Diego," he said. "Conference security is lousy. There's no way you can go."

He saw the dismay in her eyes, and the discipline with

which she controlled it. "I don't believe I asked you to call the hotel," she said carefully.

"You don't ask me to check the locks at night, either, but I wouldn't be doing my job if I let that stop me."

She brushed her hands together. They were trembling. She clasped them in front of her and said, "It is not your job to tell me what I can and cannot do." Princess to peasant.

His jaw set. "It's my job to protect you."

She raised her eyebrows. "Fine. Protect me in San Diego."

"I can't. That threat you got—it came from Los Angeles."

"Then it didn't come from Tamir," she said.

He scowled. "You don't think Kamal's men have passports?"

"I don't think Sheik Ahmed's men are involved at all," she said in her precise, maddening way. "And neither does your government, or they would have assigned other protection to me."

"You mean, instead of one broken-down, former Navy SEAL?" he asked dryly.

"Don't pretend to appeal to my sympathy, Jack. I can't imagine a man who needs pity less than you do. I *meant* your protection is certainly adequate against any threat I'm likely to face here."

He squelched a twinge of gratification—she didn't think he was pitiful; swell—and argued, "Yeah, sure. Here. You said it yourself. Montana is safe. California is a whole different ball game. Even if it was safe for you to travel—and that's a big if—San Diego is still too close to whoever sent that note."

She rolled her eyes. "Oh, please. Like some stalker's

going to drive a hundred miles down Highway 5 to hang around my hotel. No one even knows I'm going.''

Frustration ripped at him. She was going to princess herself right into a kidnapping scenario.

One stride brought him to her potting bench. He loomed over her, deliberately intimidating, trying to ignore the widening of her big blue eyes, the expensive shampoo smell of her hair. ''Uh-huh. Is your name on the conference program?''

''Well, yes, but—''

''Then they know. Anyone could get in and get at you. It's a public hotel.''

She drew herself up. The tips of her breasts almost touched his chest. She didn't even notice. He did. Too much.

''With hotel staff,'' she said. ''Hotel *security*.''

''A bunch of ex-cops and former military who draw their paychecks from some private security firm. Oh, yeah, they'll be a big help against international terrorists.'' He snorted. ''The hotel's not even adding extra staff to deal with the convention crowd.''

''These are biologists, Jack, not rugby players. I'm sure the hotel management feels their security measures are sufficient.''

Didn't she see the danger? Didn't she care? He put his face down close to hers. ''It doesn't matter how they feel. You're not going.''

Her face closed. She leaned against the potting bench and crossed her arms. ''You sound just like my father.''

He stepped back. ''Well, that's appropriate,'' he said in disgust.

She raised haughty eyebrows in question.

''You're reacting like you're about twelve years old,'' he explained.

Her shoulders squared. Her voice frosted. "Don't you try to patronize me. I've been patronized by experts."

"What the hell are you talking about? You're a damn princess."

"You don't understand," she snapped.

"Then make me," he invited. "Tell me why this trip is important enough for you to risk your life."

"Because this is what I've been working toward all my life. This is my chance to be accepted by my peers, not for how I look, not for who I was born, but for what I do."

"Why should you care? You're doing valuable research. You don't have anything to prove to them."

"But I do. I've had to prove myself every minute of every day I've worked or studied," she said bitterly. "I've heard every blonde joke that's circulated on the Internet. I've had grant applications turned down by foundations who believe that research ability is magically linked to the Y chromosome. I've had colleagues tell me my articles have been accepted for publication only because of who my father is. This symposium is the most important speaking invitation I've received. The head of my old department is a featured speaker. This is my chance to prove myself."

Jack couldn't let himself be swayed, by her arguments or her passion. He shook his head. "It's not your only chance. You have your entire career ahead of you. You shouldn't sacrifice your life to make a point."

"I'm not sacrificing anything." She risked contact, reaching out to touch his sleeve. She still had dirt on her elegant fingers. "I'm trusting you to keep me safe."

Hell. She had no idea what she was doing. What she was asking.

"What if I don't?" he asked harshly. "What if I fail?"

"You won't," she said confidently.

"I have."

Confusion clouded those confident blue eyes. "When?"

He shrugged off her touch. Turned away. He didn't want to watch her confusion turn to pity. To disgust. "Four months ago."

"In the Philippines," she guessed. "When you were wounded. But…that wasn't a failure, Jack."

He forced the words out. She deserved to know. "I was wounded after."

"After what?"

He turned back to her, the truth more painful and disabling than any scar. Now she would see the kind of man he really was. He wasn't fit to be a SEAL anymore. He wasn't fit to be trusted with anybody's safety. "I got hit after Rocky—after my swim buddy—was shot."

Chapter 12

Jack's face looked carved from stone. His eyes were dark and anguished. Christina absorbed his words, but they made no sense. "Your swim buddy?"

"My partner," he said shortly. "The guy I went through BUD/S with. The guy who covered my back and saved my butt a couple hundred times in twelve years. Rocky Garcia from Trenton, New Jersey."

"I'm sorry," she said softly. "Was he…?"

"Killed?" Jack looked away. "Yeah."

She inhaled slowly. All right. He'd lost his best friend. That was bad. But not bad enough to explain why Jack, the most confident, competent man she'd ever known, was suddenly looking uncertain. "How did it happen?"

"I wish to God I knew." He paced the tiny aisle between the rows of immature plants, moving with surprising silence in the glass enclosure. "I was point man going in. That was my job, to watch out for bad guys and booby traps. We had some terrorists up in the mountains who'd taken a schoolteacher and a classroom of kids hostage and were demanding six million dollars and three prisoners released from U.S. jails. They gave our government ten days to respond before they started beheadings. So on day five, we went in.''

She held her breath, afraid he would stop talking. Dreading what he had to say.

Jack shoved his hands deep in his pockets and hunched his good shoulder. ''We were secure going in. I brought the squad on a crawl to the tree line around the old church where they'd stashed the kids. We were secure, I swear.''

His voice was low. He almost could have been talking to himself. But Christina heard every word, and her heart twisted.

''When we reached the target, Horse and Buzz went in and neutralized the guards. We had a little firefight outside, took out maybe a dozen. When it was over, most of the squad headed out to the extraction point with the hostages. Eighteen kids, and this young schoolteacher. She was crying.''

Jack had stopped pacing. He was standing over the neat rows of tiny green plants, but his eyes were focused on something faraway and dark. ''Rocky and I stayed back. Rear security. I was taking pictures for the after-action report when they dropped Rocky. I never saw the son of a bitch who did him.''

She exhaled shakily. ''What did you do?''

''Hit the ground. Returned fire. I was crawling for Rocky, trying to drag him to cover, firing to keep down the T's—terrorists. Only they squeezed off another burst before I reached him. I got this.'' He touched his shoulder. ''And Rocky…''

His jaw worked. He did not finish his sentence. He did not need to.

"I am so sorry," Christina whispered again.

"He was a good guy," Jack said. "He deserved better."

"I'm sure you did everything you could."

"He and his wife were separated. Sally couldn't take the life, Rocky being gone on a moment's notice, her worrying when he'd get back. If he'd get back. They had a little boy. I went to see them when I got out of the hospital."

"That was nice of you."

His mouth twisted. "Yeah. She thanked me. She gave me a cup of coffee at her kitchen table. And then she asked me why I hadn't brought her husband home."

Christina recoiled. "You were wounded," she protested.

"He was my swim buddy. It was my job to bring him out. I'd dragged him maybe a quarter mile toward the extraction point when Horse came back for us. But it was too late." Jack closed his bitter blue eyes. "It was too late back at the church."

"You had to leave him," she said gently.

His eyes opened. He glared at her. "Hell, no. The SEALs have never left a dead or wounded comrade behind. But I couldn't save him."

How he had managed to move his fallen comrade at all, with his shoulder shattered and his heart pumping the blood from his body, she would never know. Could not begin to imagine. But she saw all too clearly that what she honored as an act of loyalty and courage, he dismissed as failure.

"It wasn't your fault," she stated.

"You can't know that," Jack said.

She raised her eyebrows, refusing to be intimidated by his discouraging tone. "You retired from the navy, did you not? You weren't discharged or reprimanded."

"It was my responsibility to protect him," Jack insisted

stubbornly. "In the Teams, your life literally depends on the man standing next to you. You have to be able to trust him. And I was standing next to Rocky when he died."

She bit her lip. "The rest of your squad...did they blame you?"

He stalked the short space between the tables. "I don't know."

"Well, did you talk about it?"

"No."

She sighed. "No, of course you didn't. Jack Dalton, Man of Action. Did they even come to see you in the hospital?"

Jack stiffened at this implied criticism of his squad. "Yeah. Sure."

"And?" she prompted gently.

"It didn't come up."

"It should have."

He swung around like a wounded bull, head low, eyes frustrated. "I didn't want to talk about it, all right? I don't want to talk about it now."

Right. Why would he talk to her? He wouldn't even have sex with her.

"Very well. But nothing you have said convinces me that you aren't capable of providing my protection." She lifted her chin. "I'm going to San Diego, Jack. And I would feel much safer if you would accompany me."

"And if I say no?"

Her heart rate quickened. "I'll go anyway. But I won't feel as safe."

He scowled. "You really think your father is going to let you get away with this?"

Her sister's voice whispered encouragement in her head. *When you do decide that you want something, Squidge, nothing and no one stands in your way.*

She wanted this. She needed to prove her own worth, needed Jack to accept his. And he needed to know she trusted him.

"I'm over twenty-one," she said, much more coolly than she felt. "I don't think Papa can stop me."

"I can," Jack said grimly.

It was a challenge, pure and simple. And she welcomed it, welcomed the chance to engage him on this one level, at least.

She wasn't going to isolate herself from trouble this time. She'd run from her family. From the press. From the hurt of Ryan's betrayal.

She wasn't running anymore.

She moved in front of him. "How? Are you going to tie me up?"

"I'd like to," he muttered.

Her blood pounded in her veins. Her muscles tensed for flight or fight. She could see an answering tension locking his shoulders, simmering in his eyes. It gave her hope. It gave her courage.

She took a step closer. "Try it."

A dark flush stained his cheeks. "What the hell do you want from me?"

She wasn't sure. Maybe she wanted to goad him into losing some of that awesome control. Maybe she hoped she could make him take her on. Make him take her in.

But he was too much a man for that.

Or else, she thought bleakly, she wasn't enough of a woman. Because before she could frame a response, he turned away.

"I can't let you go," he said. "Not if it means you taking unnecessary risks."

Jack was sweating, and not because of the damned range of motion exercises he was putting himself through. One more minute of Christina at close range, drilling him with those intelligent, sincere blue eyes, and he would have given her anything she wanted. Said anything she wanted. Done any damn thing she wanted. He'd barely escaped her.

Or had she just escaped him? He was ready to eat her alive. But he couldn't do that.

Jack rotated his left arm above his head, holding it in position with his right until the arm trembled and the shoulder joint screamed in agony. Christina trusted him to keep her safe.

Too damn bad he didn't trust himself.

He grunted. What a screwup. He could just imagine the old man's reaction when Jack called to report that he was escorting the princess into enemy territory.

Watch out for her. And keep her away from California.

Jack grimaced as he released the hold on his arm, counted to ten and raised it again. Yeah, this little excursion was going to go over big with the major.

At least Jack had done all he could to secure the hotel. He'd called San Diego again, changing her reservations from a modest double to two adjoining rooms on a limited-access floor. He'd made sure there were cameras in the elevator and facing her door. After twenty minutes wrangling and a few near threats, he'd even squeezed a promise from the Harborside's general manager to add a second plainclothes detective to their regular security force.

But Jack was aware that most snatches occurred when the target was in transit. Airline procedures would provide a measure of safety on their flight. But Christina would still be at risk on the hazardous trip from the airport to the hotel.

What he needed were reinforcements.

From habit, his mind went automatically to the team he

had depended on for so long, to Merlin and Horse, to Buzz and Little John. He gasped, released his hold and grimly rotated his arm again.

He couldn't call them. He wasn't one of them anymore. He'd lost his place among them when he'd let Rocky die, four months, two weeks and three lonely days ago. For all he knew, they weren't even in CONUS—Continental United States—now. But if they were...

Once lodged, the thought would not go away. The Naval Special Warfare Center in Coronado was only minutes from the San Diego International Airport. The squad could provide better security en route to Christina's hotel than the CTC, the FBI and the entire Montebellan army combined.

Jack lowered his arm and bent his head.

Did they blame you?

It didn't matter. He blamed himself. And the last thing he wanted to see was confirmation of his guilt in his friends' eyes.

The hospital visits had been bad enough. He'd been sick with grief and whacked with drugs. His buddies had been awkward and uncharacteristically silent. No way would he put them all through that kind of discomfort again. Not for himself. Not in a million years.

But for Christina...

Without giving himself a chance to think better of it, he reached for the bedside phone and punched in a number from memory.

Christina studied the tidy characters, black on white, marching like ants across her computer screen, and felt...empty. Frustrated. Dissatisfied. All her columns lined up, all her arguments were in order. Her presentation was logical, well-organized—and completely lacking in piz-zazz.

Kind of like her life.

She rubbed her eyes. Maybe she should call it quits. She wasn't making any headway on her notes tonight. She wasn't making any headway, period. And maybe it didn't matter. She might never get the chance to present her research, anyway.

And the six-foot-two obstacle standing in her way, the source of all her frustration, was Jack Dalton.

She drummed her fingers on the keyboard and then had to go back and delete a line of nonsense strokes.

Damn the man. Why did he have to be so right? Oh, she'd tried to bluff him into believing she could dispense with his protection, but there was no way she was traveling to San Diego without him. She wasn't that brave. She wasn't that foolish. She cared too much about her family and her responsibilities.

Her heart stumbled. She cared too much about Jack.

He already blamed himself for his swim buddy's death. She didn't believe in his guilt for an instant. But she simply could not risk her own safety as long as Jack might blame himself for letting her go alone into danger.

No, the more she thought about it, the more she was stuck with doing the Right Thing. The reasonable thing. The appropriate thing. Christina sighed. Her family had always been big on "appropriate." And if following the safe and proper course of action no longer held any appeal for her at all, well, that was hardly Jack's fault, now, was it?

She frowned at her computer screen. Sure it was.

"Got a problem?" Jack asked from behind her.

Christina jumped. He moved too quietly. If she wanted

to feel like she was being stalked, she'd go lock herself in the lion cage at the zoo. "With what?" she asked crossly.

He gestured toward her laptop. "Your workshop?"

"You mean, aside from the fact that you're adamantly opposed to my giving one?"

"About that..." He frowned. He put a white envelope down on the kitchen table, next to her computer. "Here. I meant to give this to you earlier."

Her heart thumped in panic. She stared at the envelope without picking it up. "What is this? Your resignation?"

He looked annoyed. "No. Disappointed?"

"Of course not. What—?"

"It's the color slides. Of the sites." When she still made no move to open it, he added, "For your presentation?"

She stiffened. Maybe he meant well, but... "I hardly think they're necessary now, do you?"

He shrugged. "Suit yourself. If you can't use them—"

"Not for the foreseeable future. Unless..." She swallowed, hardly daring to hope. "Unless you've changed your mind."

He scowled and rubbed his jaw. "I still don't think you should take unnecessary risks."

"Naturally," she agreed demurely.

He sent her a swift, suspicious look. "But as long as you're willing to take certain precautions..."

"Well, I—well, yes!" she cried, and jumped up from her chair.

It toppled backward. Jack caught it with one hand and set it right.

"Hey." He grinned. "Take it easy."

He'd just given her her heart's desire, and he wanted her to take it easy? Not likely. She hugged her arms. She wanted to hug him. Smiling, she leaned into him and saw his eyes darken and felt the rhythm of his breathing change—shallower, faster—and thought *ha! Good.*

"But this is wonderful," she said.

He looked uncomfortable. "It wasn't—"

"Thank you," she said firmly, sweetly, and stood on tiptoe to kiss him. She had to balance herself with her hands on his biceps. His muscles were like granite.

He was standing so straight and still that her first effort landed slightly astray, on the corner of his well-carved mouth. She felt him inhale once, sharply, and then his breath stopped altogether. His lips—what she could reach of them—were warm and smooth. She changed the angle of her head and kissed him again, fitting her mouth over his.

It *was* wonderful. His mouth was hot, and his jaw was rough, and he smelled so good, like soap and Jack, and this time when she leaned into him, his arms came around her and he kissed her back, hard.

Yes. She sagged, craving full contact with his body, welcoming the thrust of his tongue. Her heart was racing. His was pounding, and his chest was hard. His belly was hard. He was hard all over. She smiled against his mouth and pressed closer, flattening her breasts against the hot, solid wall of his chest.

He muttered something and buried his lips against her throat. Her head spun. Her eyes closed. He palmed her breasts through her shirt, his touch rough and possessive, and she shuddered. She wanted this, wanted him, just like this. Fast. Hot. Dangerous.

As long as you're willing to take certain precautions… Precautions.

Birth control, her sister's voice warned inside her head. *You should buy birth control.*

She jerked away just as his hands came up to catch her wrists.

Jack held her a little away from him, his breathing fast and uneven. "Whoa," he said. "Maybe you shouldn't thank me until you see them."

She blinked at him. Them? Oh, the pictures. She blushed. Of course, he meant the pictures.

"I'm sure—" Her voice scraped. She cleared her throat. "I'm sure they're fabulous."

"Yeah, well..." Her pulse thudded against his hold. He shifted his grip, moved away from her. "Maybe you should take a look at them."

She stared at him, bereft. "All right. Jack—"

Avoiding her eyes, he pulled out the chair for her. "Sit down." He handed her the envelope. "Here."

Reluctantly, she accepted the pictures. What was she supposed to do? "Are we going to talk about this?"

He took a deep breath. "No."

Her mouth curved. "Scared?" she teased.

He met her gaze then, and she jolted from the heat in his eyes.

"You bet," he said. "And if you had any sense, you would be, too. Now look at the pictures, cupcake, and I'll try really hard to forget there are three beds, a couch, and a nice rug in front of the fireplace that I could drag you to."

Her face flamed. Her stomach clenched. She didn't want to look at pictures, she thought mutinously. She wanted Jack. On the bed, yes, and on the couch and in front of the fireplace. Anywhere. Everywhere.

It only takes one time, Julia cautioned. *If you got pregnant, too, Papa would have apoplexy or something.*

Christina sighed. With trembling fingers, she peeled

back the envelope flap and slid the photos out onto the table.

But when she saw them, the pictures themselves stole her attention and her breath.

"I had them make up glossies to go with the slides," Jack said. "I figured they'd be easier for you to see."

She saw perfectly. Jack had captured each site perfectly: the desolation of the slickens, the hopeful vegetation of the mine tailings, the riot of color and life in a sun-flooded clearing. It was a record of nature's persistence, a testament to the regenerative power of the tiny bacteria Christina had given her life to studying.

She couldn't imagine a more fitting or persuasive accompaniment to her work.

"These are...excellent," she said.

He frowned over her shoulder. "I could have done better with a wider lens," he said.

"No. These are perfect. You could be a professional photographer."

He propped himself against the kitchen table, his hip close enough to her arm that she could feel his heat. He raised an eyebrow. "Taking family portraits and pictures of the bride? I don't think so."

The memory of his words echoed harshly between them. *I don't have prospects anymore.*

"I just meant that you were good enough," Christina said.

"Great. If you can use them, I'm happy. But I'm not going to pretend that deep inside me beats the heart of a frustrated photographer."

Christina lifted her chin. *Say it,* she thought. *Go for it.* Fear and daring made her dizzy. "You don't have to be frustrated. I can use whatever you give me."

He went very still. "You mean, the slides."

She moistened her lips. Okay, so she was going to have to be more direct. "The slides," she agreed, "and whatever else you want to offer me."

She could feel him tense above her. Her heart pounded hopefully. But he only said, quietly, "I'm not going to give you anything that's going to hurt you."

She attempted a smile. "I hear it only hurts the first time."

"Christina..." She looked up. His face was like flint. His eyes were dark with regret. "Don't," he said.

The biggest drawback to being direct, Christina thought numbly later, was that when things totally did not work out you couldn't blame it all on a misunderstanding. Jack had been perfectly clear. He would give her what she wanted professionally—his escort to San Diego and his slides for her presentation—but not personally. He'd made it possible for her to have everything she'd ever worked for.

But as she retreated to her room, her pride and her feet dragging, she wondered—had she lost the chance for something even more precious?

Chapter 13

"This way." Jack took Christina's elbow to lead her off the plane ahead of the rest of the passengers disembarking from Alaska Airlines flight 558 from Seattle-Tacoma to San Diego.

Last on, first off, he'd explained to her and the flight attendants. For security reasons. No one getting a look at the I'm-in-command set of his jaw was inclined to argue with him.

She let him steer her past the flight crew and down the carpeted exit ramp. It was the most contact they'd had all day. Even in his first-class seat, beside her on the aisle, Jack had kept his knees and elbows carefully to himself.

"I don't see why we didn't just keep my original reservations and fly through Denver," Christina grumbled. She had made the trip before, in the first awful weeks after Lucas's plane went down. "At least then we wouldn't be arriving here in the middle of the night."

Jack glanced down at her. "Bingo. If anybody's looking

for you, they'll expect you to fly through Denver. Besides, fewer people travel at night."

Christina covered a yawn. "That's because they don't want to be exhausted the next morning," she muttered, but Jack wasn't listening. His attention had already moved ahead, to the brightly lit terminal.

Her gaze skated along the sagging rope separating the exit ramp from the empty waiting area. Who was Jack looking for? He'd already canceled her driver.

"Are you expecting someone?" she asked.

"Not here. This is an international concourse. Only passengers are allowed through to the gates."

"Then—"

"If somebody seriously wants you, he could buy a ticket."

"If someone seriously wants me," she said significantly, looking at him, "he could ask."

But Jack pretended not to hear.

He chivied her quickly down a long hall and two escalators to the baggage claim area. "We'll get you settled and then pick up your bags."

"Why can't we get them now?"

"I don't want you out in the open."

She stopped. "Jack. I have flown before. I don't think—"

"Good. Save your thinking for the conference. Let me handle security."

She *had* agreed to cooperate. Pressing her lips together, Christina let him half guide, half drag her toward the exit.

She felt his tension before she understood its cause. His attention sharpened. His hold on her arm tightened. Christina froze.

There. By the rack of baggage carts. Was that blond giant watching them? And from the row of chairs by the sliding doors, a wiry African American male in a Padres cap put down his newspaper and came toward them.

A thrill of fear ran through her. Was Jack right? Was someone waiting for her, after all?

But then the big man's face split in a wide grin, and the thin one flashed them a quick thumbs-up, and she felt Jack relax beside her.

The thin black man reached them first. "Senior Chief," he said with obvious pleasure. "Good to see you. I've got the car outside. Norris will get your luggage."

Christina didn't mind being waited on. But, intrigued, she wanted an introduction. "Oh, please don't—"

"Christina," Jack said low in her ear. "You're a target. Now move."

She moved. Out the sliding doors. Along the concrete walk. Before she could take more than one breath of warm, moist, exhaust-laden air, she found herself in the back seat of an undistinguished dark sedan.

Only when the engine was humming and the door locks clicked did Jack perform introductions.

"Christina, may I present Information Systems Technician Second Class Lewis Johnson. Merlin, this is…" He hesitated.

"Christina Sebastiani," she supplied, offering her hand over the back of the upholstered seat.

"Pleasure, ma'am." He took her hand. His touch was light and dry, like his voice.

"Please, call me Christina. And I should call you…?"

"Merlin'll do, ma'am. Christina."

She heard the car trunk slam shut, and then the blond Arnold Schwarzenegger look-alike slid into the front seat beside him.

"Gunner's Mate First Class Bill Norris," Jack supplied.

He turned to her with a wide grin and a wider palm. "Hey."

She smiled back. "And what should I call you?"

"Norris," Jack said at the same time the man offered, "Horse."

She raised her eyebrows. "That is your nickname? You are an equestrian?"

He turned red and retrieved his hand in a hurry. "No, ma'am."

Merlin grinned as he steered the car smoothly away from the curb. "He got it on account of those silk shorts we wear in BUD/S, ma'am. To stop chafing? Well, during the medical inspection, Horse here, he—"

"That's enough," Jack snapped.

And it was. Enough for Christina to understand, at any rate. She felt her face glow as red as Bill Norris's.

"Hoo—yah, Senior," Merlin said.

"Good to have you back, Senior," Norris added.

"Not Senior. Not anymore," Jack said. "I appreciate you both coming."

"We all would have been here," Merlin said. "But Little John and the lieutenant got called to the morgue to ID a body."

Norris nodded. "Lieutenant said to tell you to count on us. For anything, anytime. Senior."

Christina's heart expanded as she absorbed the unspoken message behind the words. She wondered if Jack heard it, too. He was still one of them. Their senior chief.

"I…" Jack's voice was husky. "I appreciate it," he said again.

Tears filled Christina's eyes. But as she leaned back against the upholstered seat, listening as they started to talk in some abbreviated male code about people she didn't know and situations she could only guess at, she was smiling.

The wiry black SEAL slipped out of the penthouse-level suite and nodded once to Jack. "All secure, Senior."

"Thanks, Merlin." Jack held the door open for a pale and tired-looking Christina while Merlin grabbed a bag from Bill Norris. "Thanks to both of you."

"Hey, anytime we can hang around a gorgeous blonde's hotel room instead of the base…" Norris joked as he carried a couple of suitcases inside.

Jack scowled, his gaze slipping again to Christina. Even after six hours of travel, she wore dignity on her shoulders like a fashion scarf. The princess in her private tower. No way would she appreciate having her situation turned into a joke by a couple of sailors.

But Christina only smiled.

Norris hurried into speech. "What I meant was, you've got it made here, Senior."

"Shut up," Merlin advised. "You're only making things worse." He set the last case by the closet. "We'll clear out now. Send up a flare if you need us, Senior."

"Will do." Jack clasped hands with his former teammates. Men he had served and fought with, side by side. Men he had been afraid to face for too long, because of what he might see in their eyes. Blame. Disgust.

He looked at them now and found nothing but respect and a cautious understanding.

"Thank you both so much," Christina said.

"Ma'am. A pleasure," Merlin said.

Norris grinned and held her hand a calculated fraction too long. "Sure was nice to meet you."

"Get out of here," Jack growled.

Norris laughed. Christina bent her head and smiled.

"That was nice," she said, as the door closed behind both men.

And it had been, Jack realized with faint surprise. The awkward reunion he'd been dreading hadn't been so damn bad, after all.

Christina glided to the room's elegant half bar, her beige silk slacks whispering as she walked. They were practical for traveling, she'd told him this morning, but, watching her walk away from him, he was having definitely impractical thoughts. He couldn't see any panty lines at all under the clinging silk.

A lot of SEALs ditched wearing shorts after training. So maybe Christina did have something in common with his buddies. Maybe she wasn't wearing underwear, either.

He felt the temperature in the climate controlled room climb about a hundred degrees. His face flushed.

"Are you warm? Can I get you something to drink?" she asked.

"No. Thanks." He should go. He would go, in just a minute.

Ice cubes rattled in a glass. She poured club soda over them. Someone had taken the time to fill the ice bucket for her, to stock the bar. He'd requested the best the hotel had to offer, only thinking of the improved security money could buy.

But now, watching Christina make herself at home, he couldn't help but contrast her luxury accommodations with his cheap little motel room in Billings. He could never afford a place like this on his disability pay.

Of course, he didn't have to, he thought wryly. King Papa was paying for it.

Still, Christina could end up costing Jack more than a mere four hundred dollars a night. A regular Joe like him couldn't afford to get involved with her.

"I like your friends," she said, observing him over the rim of her glass. "They weren't quite what I was expecting."

"Yeah? What were you expecting?"

She lifted one shoulder, faintly embarrassed. Her sweater pulled across her breast. He looked away. "I'm not sure. Superman, perhaps?"

He rubbed his jaw. "Well, Norris kind of resembles the Terminator."

She laughed, a low ripple of amusement that detonated inside him like a homemade bomb. He really ought to go.

"Actually, I was thinking of Clark Kent," she said. "The man of steel in disguise? In the airport...I didn't even notice them at first."

"We do covert ops, princess. We're not supposed to stand out."

"But you do," she said softly. "You're not like anyone I've ever known."

He broke out in a sweat. He so did not want to hear this. She didn't know what she was saying. She was tired, and he was near the end of his tether. One more inviting smile and his control would snap, and he'd be all over her like a drug-sniffing dog on a kilo of contraband.

"Well, you just met two more of me. The new, improved version. Younger, faster, stronger." He smiled wryly. "The kind that comes with a job and a full complement of working parts."

Christina's glass clinked on the marble counter. "You know, I'm getting a little tired of rejection, Jack. How many working parts do you need, anyway?"

"For what, princess? You want me to kiss you? I can do that. You want me to hold you? I can do that, too. You want to screw the help, I've got the parts and the inclination, but one of us is going to hate me for it."

She trembled. He saw, and hated himself already.

"That was blunt," she said.

"I'm a blunt kind of guy. At least this way you're protected."

"Protected from what?"

"Disappointment."

She threw up her hands. Let them fall. "What do you call this?"

"Doing my job," he answered grimly.

"Well, fine. Do your job. I have a workshop tomorrow morning at ten o'clock in the Alta Vista Room. Check for bombs, sweep for bugs, alert the staff and watch out for intruders." She shook her blond hair away from her face and lifted her chin. "And lock your bedroom door, Jack, because I must be protected at any cost."

It was over, Christina thought.

And it had gone fabulously well.

Martin Kauffman, chairman of her old department at UCLA, patted her on the arm and then stepped back, beaming like a balding Santa Claus.

"—excellent examples of the potential for beneficial bacteria to enhance receptivity of root systems," he was saying.

Christina glowed. "Thank you. Although I really didn't have time to expand on indirect interactions—the benefits to mycorrhizal fungi, for example—as much as I would have liked."

"I would have enjoyed that," Kauffman said regretfully. "You know, you should consider paying our department a little visit. We haven't finalized our speaker program for the fall. I'll have Sinan give you a call, if you're interested."

Interested? She was thrilled.

"Who will call?"

"Sinan Omer. He was a few years ahead of you, stayed on to do disease studies. Do you remember him?"

She concentrated until she had a face, thin and arrogant behind wire-rimmed glasses, to go with the name.

Apologetically, she said, "Not well, I'm afraid."

"No matter." Kauffman twinkled. "You have other claims on your time and attention, I'm sure. Perhaps you'll introduce your old teacher to your new young man?"

She was confused. "To...?"

"Time to go," Jack said in her ear.

Heat bloomed in her cheeks. Had he been there all along? What had he heard?

His hand was warm and strong on her back. "Say good-bye to the professor," he instructed.

She felt like a six-year-old banished from her own birthday party. "Not now," she whispered. "I just finished talking. People are still coming up."

"Too many people, too damn close. I want you out of this crowd. Now."

Frustration left a flat taste in her mouth. She swallowed. "All right," she said evenly, and turned back to the department chairman. "Dr. Kauffman—"

"Please. Marty."

She smiled. "Marty. I'm afraid something's come up. But I appreciate you coming to hear my talk. And I hope you were serious about the possibility of my speaking this fall."

Marty Kauffman bobbed his round, bald head. "Absolutely. Sinan will get in touch with you the minute we're back in L.A. I was sorry when we lost you to Montana. You were one of the best students I ever had. A credit to the department."

It was vindication on a level she had longed for and never expected.

"Well...thank you. I—"

"Upstairs," Jack said, rough and low.

She didn't want to go upstairs. She wanted to stay right here while Dr. Kauffman—Marty—told her how clever she was. But she had promised Jack her cooperation. So she made her excuses, made her farewells, made her way to the private elevator with Jack a protective two steps behind.

She stared straight ahead as the elevator doors closed, mentally rehearsing her response when Sinan Omer called.

"Don't sulk."

Startled, she met Jack's amused blue eyes in the mirrored wall.

"I wasn't sulking, I was thinking," she said with dignity.

"Well, don't overdo it," he advised. "You done good."

"You mean, coming along quietly when you dragged me off?" she asked.

"I meant your talk. You were very clear. Very cool."

"Thank you," she said politely. And then ruined the effect by adding, "How would you know, anyway? You barely looked at me."

"I was watching the room. But I managed to take a few shots for your scrapbook. And I heard you. You wowed them, cupcake."

Pleasure suffused her chest. She turned. "Really?"

He nodded, his eyes warm and steady on hers. "Really. You sure impressed the hell out of me."

And he bent his head to kiss her, warmly, briefly, in congratulation.

All the nerves and excitement she had felt all day crashed inside her. Relieved that he was kissing her at all, she twined her arms around his neck and pulled his head back down, her fingers combing through his short hair to learn the shape of his skull, to find the beat of blood under his skin. Like a scientist with some rare discovery, she wanted to observe, to explore, to experiment. She wanted him.

Desire slugged Jack like a fist. She was so warm. So eager. His breath went. His entire body clenched. She burned in his arms, fire and ice, her glowing eyes, her demanding mouth, her hot body. Her tongue teased his, and his control went up in flames.

He reached over her head and did something quick and complicated to the control panel. The elevator jerked to a halt between floors.

He leaned into her heavily and kissed her hard. She made a soft, assenting sound and wiggled to adjust her body to his. All the blood left his brain and surged into his groin. He had to feel her, had to… Filling his hands with her bottom, he kneed her legs apart, pushed into the vulnerable crux of her thighs. Deliberately, he rubbed against her, shuddering with satisfaction when she moaned.

Yes, he thought, and did it again, the fullness of his arousal making a mockery of their clothes. She tipped her hips into his, and he sucked in his breath sharply.

She pulled back, biting her lower lip. Her mouth was swollen. Her hair fell in strands across her flushed face. He could have her, he thought. Take her, here. He ached to take her.

"Jack…"

He forced his hands to be still, his voice to respond. "What?" he growled.

Her color deepened. "Do you want to wait? Until we get to the room?"

"No," he said hoarsely. He tried to remember why. "I don't trust myself in your room."

Her brows drew together. "Trust yourself to do what?"

"To stop," he explained.

"For heaven's sake, why?"

Under the prodding of her voice, he tried to organize his thoughts, but they were still focused on her, on her full mouth, her soft breasts, her hot little, heart-shaped rear end....

He shook his head. "We couldn't count on being interrupted in your room."

"We wouldn't be interrupted here," she snapped. "You stopped the elevator."

Silently, he pointed to the camera mounted in the upper corner.

"Oh, *no*." She covered her face with her hands. Belatedly, he remembered her dislike of having her picture taken. "Did you know all along that was there?" she asked, her voice muffled.

He wished he could lie to her. He nodded, forgetting for the moment that she couldn't see. "Yes," he said.

She raised her head. He expected her to be mortified. But her face was composed and cold. Only her hurt and angry eyes gave her away.

"You son of a bitch," she said clearly.

Jack was shocked. Shaken. He'd never heard her swear before. "Christina—"

"Don't you 'Christina' me. I'm tired of you treating me like the Virgin Princess of Montebello. And the one time I'm woman enough to get under your thick skin, you've got video cameras and a security guard to make sure I don't get away with it."

"I'm only trying to protect you, damn it."

"So you've said. Has it occurred to you that the last

thing I need in my life is one more paternalistic male convinced he has the right to decide what is in my best interests? As if I couldn't decide for myself. As if I were some sexless, brainless thing.''

He never imagined she would take his care of her that way. ''Look, I think you're overreacting here. Why don't we have dinner, and—'' Oh, hell. Manfully, he continued. ''—and we can talk.''

''I don't want to have dinner with you. I don't want to talk with you.'' She lifted her chin and squared her shoulders. ''In fact, I'm not sure I'm even speaking to you anymore.''

Chapter 14

Jack thumped a pillow behind his head and scowled at the door connecting his room with Christina's. Locked on his side, almost certainly locked on hers.

He surfed through the channels on the hotel TV. Nothing on but the evening news and old sitcoms, auto racing and some movie with a bunch of women complaining about their loser boyfriends while the pretty one died slowly of a protracted illness. He tossed down the remote in disgust.

So he could lie here and think about sex with Christina, which made him hot and uncomfortable. Or he could think about arguing with Christina, which made him angry and uncomfortable.

Some choice. He didn't want to think at all.

A memory of Christina's cool, dry voice intruded on his sulks. *A real man of action.*

Yeah. So why the hell was he lying here?

He hadn't seen any action since the Philippines. Hadn't

had any action since…that enthusiastic aerobics instructor in Galveston, he guessed. Deliberately, he tried to summon a memory of that encounter with Krystal, but all that would come to him were sharp, hot images of Christina's swollen mouth. Christina's shining eyes. Christina's body, snug and warm against his. He thought about what had happened in that elevator, and he thought about what would have happened if he hadn't stopped, and that was a really bad idea, because he was going out of his mind.

He rolled off the bed. This was why he shouldn't think. All he could think about was Christina.

All he wanted was Christina. Not just her body under his, but her dry wit and her sharp intelligence and her strong passion for her work, for life, for him. *Maybe I want your soul, Christina.* Hell, yes. He could imagine wanting her forever, and he was not a forever kind of guy.

The last thing a dedicated, intelligent, professional woman like Christina needed was to get mixed up with a rough, tough, former military Joe with a bad shoulder and no prospects. He was paid to protect her. He would die before he hurt her.

He stopped pacing, brought up short by the hotel wall and his own realization.

He'd hurt her already.

There had been real hurt behind the anger simmering in her eyes. *I'm tired of you treating me like the Virgin Princess of Montebello.*

Wasn't that what her former boyfriend had done, that Cunningham character? Defined her, limited her, put her in a box labeled Princess: Do Not Touch. And now Jack, with the best of intentions, had done the same. No wonder she'd been pissed off. And hurt.

He rubbed his jaw and eyed the connecting door again. He might have lost his shoulder and his career, but he hadn't lost the experience gained in fourteen years in ports of call. He knew what he could do for her. In this one area, at least, he could give her the royal treatment. But to do that, he needed to see her, damn it. Needed to talk to her.

Only Christina wasn't speaking to him right now. And he had a strong suspicion that if he broke the door down to offer her an apology and sex, she wasn't going to yell "hooray" and start taking off her clothes.

A rap sounded on the metal security door, cleverly built up with plaster and gilt to look like something from the Marquise de Pompadour's boudoir.

"Room service," a male voice called.

Christina lifted her head from her pillow. Her dinner was here. And if her Triple Chocolate Decadence wasn't on the cart, the waiter would have to die. She already had to do without Jack and sex. She wasn't giving up chocolate, too.

Swiping angrily at her wet eyes with her fingertips, she scrambled off the mattress and strode to the door.

She had the chain half off before she remembered she was the supposed target of kidnappers, and looked through the peephole.

Jack.

Her poor heart squeezed. And then she rallied. If she couldn't kill the waiter, Jack would do nicely.

She straightened her shoulders and opened the door. "What's this?"

"Dinner." He eyed her warily as he wheeled the cart into the room. "And an apology. Which do you want first?"

She raised her chin another notch. "I only remember asking for dinner."

His eyes glimmered with what could have been admiration. Or annoyance. He positioned the serving cart in front of the green-and-white-striped silk couch and removed the silver tray covers. His eyebrows rose. "Did you really order three desserts?"

She felt the blood rise in her face. "Triple Chocolate Decadence, chocolate mousse, and raspberries and cream. Do you have a problem with that?"

"Nope."

"I'm certainly old enough to order what I want."

He nodded slowly. "Yeah. I get that now."

She stopped on her way to the couch, suddenly uncertain. "Are we still talking about my triple hit of chocolate?"

"That, and other choices you have a right to make for yourself." He looked at her, his navy blue eyes dark and direct. She felt the pull of attraction low in her stomach and pressed a hand under her ribs.

"I blew it earlier, okay?" he said quietly. "I'm sorry. I'd like to make it up to you."

She narrowed her eyes, suspicious. "Make it up to me how?"

He came around the cart, toward her. "I brought you dessert."

"The waiter was bringing me dessert."

"Yeah, but would he feed you?"

A little thrill ran down the back of her neck, the backs of her arms. She hugged them across her chest. *Feed her?* "No one has fed me since I was a baby."

He stopped in front of her, close enough that she could feel his body heat. "There's a first time for everything. Maybe this is yours."

"My first?" she croaked.

His mouth quirked, but his eyes were deadly serious. "Yeah. Let me be your first, Christina."

Her heart lurched. "Why?"

"Because I want to. Because you want me to." He shrugged. "Because I like being the one you turn to when you need something."

"Like protection," she said flatly.

"Or food."

"Or sex? 'All part of the service,' isn't that what you said? Only I don't want to be served, Jack. I want to be—"

Loved, she almost said. Her breath caught in her chest. She wanted him to love her.

She exhaled shakily. "—treated like an intelligent, adult woman."

"I can treat you like a woman," he growled, and tugged her close.

Her crossed arms rested against his chest. Their lower bodies angled together. His thighs brushed hers.

He smiled down at her hot face and said, "Open your mouth."

She frowned. "Wha—?"

But before she could close her teeth on the final consonant, his hand came up from the dessert tray and he put his forefinger—his *finger*—in her mouth. She drew back instinctively, her lips closing, her tongue pushing, and tasted...chocolate.

Her body jerked in surprise. Her heart spurted in excitement.

He ran the rough, wet pad of his finger over her lower lip.

She shivered. "What are you doing?"

"Feeding you."

"But—" She saw his hand approaching, another taste of chocolate mousse on the tip of his finger, and stopped.

He held the creamy treat to her mouth. She licked her lips. Food sex. Pretty exotic fare for a virgin research scientist. She'd expected—well, she didn't know what she'd expected, but not this. Neither heavy groping in a sleeping bag or a quick, hot tumble on her bed had prepared her for this.

Sex was serious. Wasn't it?

"I was taught never to play with my food," she said.

Jack watched her, humor and heat in his eyes, and fun with food was suddenly awfully appealing.

"First time for everything," he said again.

It was a challenge. It was a dare, and everything that was determined and rebellious in her rose to take it. She closed her eyes and opened her mouth and took him inside her.

Sweet. The chocolate melted, rich and creamy against her palate. His skin was salty and warm and rough. She trapped his finger between her teeth, sucking gently, and was rewarded by his sharp intake of breath.

She let her tongue taste and explore, let her arms slip down his chest and her hands slide up his back. He had such an incredible body, lean-muscled, hard. He withdrew his finger slowly and reached behind her, leaning into her. Hard. Yes.

Maybe he didn't love her, she thought. But he wasn't lying when he said he wanted her.

She tipped back her head and waited, lips parted, eyes closed, for him to tease her again with exotic, erotic tastes of chocolate decadence. And then his mouth took sudden, full possession of hers, and she didn't think anymore.

He sampled her like she was dessert, ate her up in great big bites that fed her own hunger. He bit her lip and soothed the sting with his tongue, feasted on her throat and made her moan. Distracting her with his urgent mouth, he twined his fingers with hers. Something cool touched her fingertips. She barely noticed until he brought their joined hands up level with her chin.

Three of her fingers were coated with whipped cream.

"Feed me," he commanded hoarsely.

Oh. Her body tightened, her knees weakened at the hunger in his eyes, at the rasp in his voice. Could she?

"I don't—"

"If you want to stop," he rasped, "we'll stop. But tell me now."

Her pulse thundered. She could see his beating in the hollow under his strong jaw. She could go on hiding in her safe tower. Or she could take a running leap off the balcony and count on this battered warrior to catch her.

Slowly, she lifted her hand to his mouth. Holding her gaze, he suckled gently on her fingers. They both shuddered.

She fed him again, her breath quick and shallow as she felt the tug of his mouth on her fingers, the draw of him in her womb. He fed her. They fed each other, tiny bites of dense, dark chocolate interspersed with creamy mousse and tart berries and slow, wet kisses.

He peeled back her collar and set his teeth against the column of her throat. He pushed back the panels of her blouse to nuzzle her breast. She arched back over his arm, and he licked under the thin silk of her bra and devoured her.

She pushed at his shirt. His skin was smooth and hot. And then her questing hands slid over a ragged ridge of flesh, and he flinched.

She froze. "Did I hurt you?"

"No. No, but it's…" He straightened. His eyes were cool and blank. "The scar is pretty ugly."

She relaxed. "But it's not still sore?"

"Not now." But when her hand glided along his shoulder, he caught and held it tightly. "Maybe you'd be more comfortable if I left my shirt on."

She remembered: even when he'd had her bare on her bed, he'd stayed fully dressed. Not to exploit her weakness, she realized suddenly, but to protect his. She melted. But how could she tell him his scars didn't matter?

She smiled, hoping he would read the warmth in her eyes as desire and not pity. "Maybe *you'd* be more comfortable," she teased. "I want you naked."

His chest expanded with his breath. He stiffened as she slowly tugged on his shirt, as she slowly uncovered his shoulder, but he did not try to stop her.

The scar was big—at least three inches across. And deep—maybe half an inch gouged out of the hard curve of his arm. And wine-red and waffled from the skin graft. Visible marks from sutures marched along the edge.

She thought of what he had survived, what he had endured, what he must have felt, and tears thickened her throat.

"Told you it was ugly," he said in the face of her continued silence.

"Not ugly," she said.

Not in her eyes. It was a mark of his courage, a badge of his strength. It was part of him, like his blunt assurance or his prowling walk or the perception in his dark-blue eyes. And so she kissed the line of Frankenstein stitches and the purple, waffled scar. She kissed his collarbone and his warm, strong neck. He smelled delicious. She stood on tiptoe to kiss his chin, and his breath exploded, and he reached for her.

He sank with her on the silk-and-down cushions of the couch and did things with his hands. He did things with his mouth. He did things with the sweet cream and chocolate from the tray beside them until she thought with the tattered remnants of her mind that she would never again look at a berry without blushing. He touched her at her center and at her heart, licked, sucked and stroked her, until heat shimmered through her and she stretched and clutched and cried out his name.

When he moved over her, his body hot and urgent, her heart stood still with wonder. He was so beautiful. So beautifully made, so amazingly male.

And hers. For now, in this moment, he was hers.

But even as she arched to take him, her sister's caution nagged at her.

"I b-bought..." Christina stammered. "At the airport..."

Would he even wear a condom? She had read some men didn't like them.

He kissed her forehead. "I'll take care of it."

She relaxed. Of course he would. Jack would always protect her.

She waited while he grabbed his discarded jeans. Anticipation tensed her stomach. She knew what was going to happen. She wasn't totally naive. And she wanted him, wanted his full, fierce possession, desperately. But all her book knowledge and all her desire hadn't prepared her for the sight of him, large and hard and dark, kneeling over her....

He covered himself and then moved between her legs. She spread them to take him. A cushion slithered to the carpet. The soft silk was cool and smooth against her back. Jack was hot and unyielding against her thighs, nudging her belly.

She bit her lip. "Maybe I'm not ready."

"Yes," he said. "You are."

And in one smooth thrust, he was there, inside her, all

the way inside. She felt the shock of it in her body, saw the shock of it in his eyes.

He braced his arms by her head. "Okay?"

"I'm fine," she said breathlessly, because it was true. Amazing. She ran her hands over his damp back and tilted her hips to him.

He groaned and started moving, in and out. Her hands gripped his biceps, moved to his back. In and out. Her breath caught. Their eyes held. And still he moved, on her and in her, beyond challenge and play, beyond laughter and heat, beyond his command and her deepest, most secret yearnings.

He pushed them both to their limits and into the unknown dark, like a man going into the earth after the sparkling ore at the rock's heart. She felt it twisting and sparkling along all her veins, felt it shatter and cascade at his touch.

She cried out. "Jack!"

And like a blind fool in the mines, he lost himself and found…treasure.

He'd only meant to make her feel better.

So, okay, Jack was pretty damn sure going in that helping Christina feel better would make him feel great, too, but his motives were mostly—partly—at least a little bit pure.

He stared up at the plastered ceiling, the gilding gleaming faintly from the gray light beyond the heavy drapes.

Anyway, she was satisfied, wasn't she? And he was…out of his mind. The grinding load of frustration gone. His body felt loose and relaxed. He turned his head to study Christina's sleeping face, her pale, level brows, her cheeks pink with sleep and wrinkled from the pillow, and a stupid warmth flooded his chest and a dumb grin stretched his mouth at the thought of her, warm and wet and strong and naked, demure and enthusiastic all at once.

The best sex he'd ever had. A fantasy come true. The things they had done… But there was no way he was a match for the educated, dedicated princess anywhere but in bed.

Which didn't stop him from wanting her. Even after he'd taken her—three times last night—he wanted her again.

He wanted her for always.

His mind shuddered away from the thought even as he reached for her, even as he captured a strand of her hair, still damp from their shower, and moved it away from her lips. They curved, and he looked up from her lush pink mouth to find her awake and watching him. Her eyes smiled, shy and aware.

Lust energized his sleepy, sated body. Possessiveness clamped his heart. *Mine,* he thought, and had to force himself to release her hair and move his hand away.

This wasn't about him, what he needed, what he wanted. This was about her. He wasn't going to cramp her style at her professional conference. He wasn't going to stand in her way.

"Good morning," she said, her voice husky.

He almost jumped her. "G'morning." He cleared his own throat. "What's on the schedule for today?"

Confusion clouded those wonderful, clear blue eyes. She blinked. "Well, I—I don't really have any plans. Workshops start at nine. Dr. Kauffman is speaking this morning on the ecological limitations of nitrogen-fixing bacteria."

"You won't want to miss that." He tried to sound alert. ____y. He could have been a damn cheerleader. ___e?"

I think. Jack—"

If he didn't leave now, he would keep her in bed all morning. "Right. I'll get out of your hair, then."

He swung his legs off the side of the mattress, trying not to notice how the covers pulled against the curve of her hip, the slope of her breast. Just above the line of the sheet, there was a red mark on her white skin where he'd sucked.... He looked away hastily. Where were his pants?

He stalked to the outer room, collecting his clothes. The contents of the serving cart were scattered beside the green-and-white-striped couch. He shook his head. Housekeeping was going to have a field day in here. He tugged on his jeans, stacked a couple of plates and grabbed a couple of condom wrappers and a linen napkin from the floor. Too late to do anything about the upholstery.

Christina came out while he was sitting on the couch, tying his shoes. She was wrapped in a white hotel robe and looked fresh and clean as snow in the morning. He felt his insides twist with hunger.

"You need shoes to go back to your room?" Her voice was amused.

Something inside him relaxed. She wasn't upset, wasn't going to subject them both to the big Morning After scene.

"My door's locked," he explained.

Her smooth brows rose. "And you forgot your key."

"No, I remembered the key card." He grinned and shrugged. "I forgot to unbolt the door on my side."

She smiled, but faintly. The echo of her words rose between them. *And lock your bedroom door, Jack, because I must be protected at any cost.*

"Anyway," he said heartily, already on his way, "I'll just get into some clean duds and then meet you."

"You know where to find me," Christina said with dignity. "The door's always open...on this side."

It was an invitation he couldn't afford to accept. She

had places to go and people to see, and he had— He didn't have anything. Except the responsibility of keeping her safe.

She'd followed him to the hall door. He bent his head and gave her a brief, hard kiss.

"Lock up behind me," he instructed, and opened the door.

He saw the flash and moved to protect her even before his ears registered the whir, before his mind identified the threat.

A camera.

Some bozo with a camera had just taken Jack's picture as he left the Princess of Montebello's hotel room.

And the princess herself, her damp hair down her back and her pale skin showing in the open V of her robe, was in clear view behind him.

Chapter 15

Jack acted. That's what a SEAL was trained to do, act. Without thought or hesitation, he lunged for the nearest intruder. Male, short, chunky, vaguely familiar. Grabbing the guy's shirt, Jack reached to knock the camera from his hands.

No camera.

He dropped Chunky and sprinted after intruder number two. But the photographer was already inside the waiting elevator at the end of the hall. Jack reached the elevator doors just as they closed.

He swore and whirled on the white-faced short guy.

"Who the hell are you?" he growled.

But he already knew. He recognized him as the waiter from last night, the guy he'd bribed to hand over the dessert cart, using the princess's security as his excuse.

Damn, damn, damn.

This guy was toast.

Jack drew back his arm. His good arm.

"Jack!"

Christina stood in the door of her room, her hand at her throat, holding the lapels of her robe closed. "It's all right. I'm all right."

"This guy sold you out to some goddamn paparazzo."

Her face was pale but composed. "That makes him a nuisance, not a threat. You don't have to hit him."

"What if I want to hit him?" Jack muttered, but he lowered his fist.

"Who does he work for?" Christina asked.

"The hotel," Jack said in disgust. "He's a waiter."

"No, I meant the photographer."

Chunky—either in gratitude for her intervention or because Jack still had a tight hold of his shirt—spoke up. "Nobody. He's, like, freelance, you know?"

So her image could go anywhere. Be sold to anyone.

"I want his name and phone number," Jack said.

"I don't—" Chunky squeaked as Jack shifted his grip. "Toby Marshall. His number...I don't know it, not offhand, but he's in the phone book."

"I want yours, too," Jack said grimly.

"How come? I didn't do—"

"So I can get your butt fired, moron."

Christina cleared her throat. "I'll report him to the management, Jack. You can let him go."

"Name and phone number," Jack rapped.

Chunky gabbled out the information, and Jack let him go. Disgusted, he watched as the waiter scurried to the elevator.

"You should have let me hit him. I gave him a twenty last night."

Christina smiled, but her gaze was serious and uncertain. "Regrets, Jack?"

"About last night?" He took two strides back to her

door. She wasn't a tiny woman—around five seven, he judged—but in her bare feet, with her hair streaming down her back like a girl's, she looked small enough to fit into a man's pocket. To squeeze into his heart. "Hell, no. Unless you do."

He prayed she didn't. And maybe his luck had changed, because she shook her head.

"No regrets." She straightened her spine and looked him straight in the eye, and there wasn't a woman in the world he admired more. "I don't think a woman should ever regret dessert," she said.

The two-story hotel lobby was crowded with drifting tourists and roving conventioneers. A security nightmare.

Buzz had promised Jack backup by midafternoon, but for most of the day his old team was hung up in training exercises. Jack figured he'd be grateful if the worst his princess faced between now and then were pushy photographers and aggressive biologists.

Although Christina seemed to be handling both okay without him.

He stood five feet away—far enough to spot a threat, close enough to intervene physically if needed—and listened while she simultaneously fielded questions from a petty officer type and evaded the man's friendly little pats on her arm. Jack didn't know which he wanted more, to applaud her or bust the guy's jaw.

Christina, he figured, wouldn't thank him for either one.

So he rocked on his heels and scanned the room and tried not to think about Christina shuddering and warm and wet under him. Yeah, he wouldn't think of that at all. Wouldn't remember her neat, short nails digging into his arms, or the soft, choked cry she made at the back of her throat…ah, hell.

He rubbed his jaw. Even with her clothes on and her research scientist face firmly in place, she compelled his attention. And he wasn't the only one in the hotel lobby staring. Damn.

She stood in front of a froufrou French table, against a background arrangement of orchids and palm fronds. In this crowd of grown-up dweebs and high functioning dorks, she stuck out like a swan in a flock of gulls. He ought to be used to the masculine double takes, the bold once-overs and the sneaky peeks by now. He wondered if she was. He wondered if she ever could be, or if the relentless male inspection was one of the things that had driven her to Montana.

Jack scowled.

She was way too obvious a target.

He did another slow pan of the space, from the marble foyer in front of the reception desk to the bellhop station by the bank of elevators, over the conversational groupings of chairs and the knots of chatting conference goers around the bar. His gaze skimmed the mezzanine balcony overlooking the lobby before traveling on to the wide, carpeted stairway at the other end.

Something in the picture nagged at him, and he went back for a more careful look.

There. Up on the mezzanine, leaning over the balcony. A slight, dark man in a long-sleeved white shirt, with a red ball cap half shielding his face. He wasn't staring nearly as obviously as half of the men in the lobby, wasn't close enough to be considered a snatch threat. But something about him stirred an "uh-oh" feeling in Jack's gut.

He was already moving to hustle Christina to the elevators when the man raised his arm and fired.

Christina stood discussing indigenous ecosystems with two of the top research scholars on the West Coast, and all she could think about was Jack and raspberries and the slide of flesh on flesh. She could see him out of the corner of her eye, competent and solid, and every time she did, her heart gave a little lurch of lust and—and something else, and she lost the thread of the conversation entirely.

Oh, for pity's sake.

She was not the lustful, lost-in-wonder type. She was the logical, weigh-the-risks, minimize errors, play-it-safe type. She didn't lose her head over the promise of sex in a man's voice or the promise of forever in his eyes. Especially not a man like Jack Dalton, a sailor who had a lover in every port, a wounded warrior who made it clear he could provide her with sex but not the home her heart craved.

No, Christina of Montebello wasn't the type to lose her head and her heart over a man like Jack.

She frowned. Of course, up until last night, she'd never imagined she was the chocolate decadence type, either, and he had certainly proved her wrong there.

One of her companions touched her arm to make a point. "—wouldn't you agree, Dr. Sebastiani?"

She blinked. Agree? To what? Her esteemed colleague could be suggesting sex in the hotel lobby, and she wouldn't have a clue until he started removing his clothes.

She winced. Horrible image. She threw out some comment about species diversity, just to prove she hadn't lost her place in the conversation, and glanced back at Jack.

She was aware of him with every fiber of her body, as if their joining had somehow imprinted her every cell. He wasn't even paying attention to her, she thought with a pinch of indignation. He was watching something on the mezzanine level above.

So she really didn't expect Jack to launch himself suddenly across the yard or so separating them and tackle her to the ground like an American football player. She hit the green-figured carpet with a whomp, Jack's hard arm beneath her, his hard body on top of her. The air whooshed out of her lungs.

And then the vase above her head shattered, and water and orchids rained down on her, and she sucked in her breath and screamed.

"Shut up," Jack ordered. He crushed her to the wet carpet, his big body bruising. "Stay down."

Shouts and cries echoed through the lobby. Her heart beat wildly as dirty water dripped from the Louis XV table onto her face, her hair. She lay still. Cowering.

Sebastianis did not cower.

She raised her head from the carpet. "What is it? What happened?"

"Gunshot," Jack said, close to her ear. "Twenty millimeter. Somebody shot at you from the mezzanine."

The intermittent buzz of an alarm—it sounded like a fire alarm—cut through the rising din.

"Help!"

"What happened?"

"Where'd he go?"

"Call the police!"

Christina pushed against Jack's chest. "Is anyone hurt?"

He shoved her head back down. "I don't know. Are you hit?"

"I don't know." She took a cautious inventory. Her lip stung. Her back ached. She would have a bump on her head by morning. "No." She struggled to sit up.

"Okay." He levered off her slightly.

Above them, Dr. Felix Ungarro of the Running Waters

Research Station bent over cautiously. "Dr. Sebastiani? Are you all right?"

She had orchids in her hair and blood on her lip and a large, angry man sprawled on top of her body. "I'm fine," she said reassuringly.

"Stay down," Jack growled.

"Are you going after him?" Christina asked.

"No."

She was bewildered. "Why not? If anyone can catch him—"

"I have to stay with you," he said shortly.

The man of action was reduced to playing baby-sitter. And he hated it. She could tell.

"I'm fine."

"Good. I'm supposed to make sure you stay that way."

"And what about everyone else? Jack, if some man with a gun is out there—"

"He could be a decoy. If I leave you, it could be the chance somebody else is waiting for to grab you."

"But someone has to go for the police," Christina objected.

Under the staccato buzz of the alarm, through the babble of frightened, angry voices, came the rising wail of sirens.

"I don't think we have to worry about that," Jack drawled.

"I'd like to know why the hell you didn't seal off this hotel when you had the chance," Jonathan Dalton said from behind the bar in Christina's hotel suite. He'd arrived less than an hour ago by private jet, and he'd already set up the bar area as a sort of command post.

The impeccably dressed San Diego police detective— Detective Martinez, Christina thought his name was— struggled visibly for patience. "We blocked all entrances as soon as we arrived on the scene, Mr. Dalton. And may I remind you again, sir, that you are not in charge of this investigation? I am."

"For now," Jonathan said heavily. "I've spoken with your captain. And the feds, who aren't going to stand by while you screw up."

She closed her eyes. Her suite had been taken over shortly after the shooting. She was tired of men's voices, tired of the ringing phone, tired of explaining who she was and what she was doing at a biology symposium. Sometime during her interview, Jack's SEAL buddy, Norris, had put in an appearance and been briefed by Jack in her bedroom. The hotel manager was sitting with the head of the private firm that provided hotel security on the couch where she'd made love with Jack. They had ordered rolls and trays of cold cuts—she wasn't hungry—and turned on the television to see if her shooting had made the evening news. The set flickered mutely. If she closed her eyes, she wouldn't have to watch.

Jack said with an edge to his voice, "When you two are done with the pissing match, do you mind if we get on with this? The princess has had a long day."

"Sorry, sweetheart." Jonathan sounded fatherly and genuinely contrite.

The hotel manager stirred on the couch. "Our apologies. Can I get you a sandwich, your, um—"

"Dr. Sebastiani." She peeked at the silver serving dishes laid out on the table. Memory flashed hotly through her. *I'm certainly old enough to order what I want.*

"No," she said, the blood rising in her face. "Thank you."

"So, did you find the gun yet?" Jack asked.

Detective Martinez's mouth tightened. "Yes, we found it. For all the good it will do us."

"Where was it?"

Martinez hesitated.

"They found it under some towels in the hamper of a utility cart," the security expert answered for him. "Up on the seventh floor. Anybody going by in the hall could have ditched the gun at any time."

"Did you question the maid?" Jonathan Dalton asked.

"She was in and out of rooms," Martinez replied. "She doesn't remember anybody hanging around the cart."

Jack rubbed his jaw. "No man in a red cap?"

"We found the ball cap stashed in a potted plant by the second floor elevator," Martinez said. "And the rest of your description—a slight, dark male in a white shirt—fits a hundred guests and fifty men who work here."

The hotel manager drew himself up. "I'm sure the princess's attacker wasn't a member of our staff."

Christina saw Jack and Bill Norris exchange glances.

"Right," Jack said. "What about guests? Conference attendees?"

Martinez tugged on his perfectly knotted tie. "We're questioning people, of course. But—"

"The police have the full cooperation of the Harborside Hotel," the manager interjected. "But, naturally, we need to protect the rights of our guests."

Jack wheeled on him. "Yeah? What about protecting Christina?"

The manager flushed. "Of course, the princess's safety is our first consideration. Hotel security—"

"Hotel security let a damn photographer up to her room this morning," Jack snapped. "Don't talk to me about hotel security."

The security expert put down his ham sandwich. "We followed protocol. If you want personal—"

Jonathan Dalton cut him off with a wave. "What's this about a photographer?"

Norris paused expectantly as he piled meat on a roll, barely keeping his broad grin in check.

Christina's stomach sank. No regrets, she'd told Jack this morning. But faced with five pairs of interested, assessing male eyes, it was remarkably difficult to go into the details of her early morning rendezvous. What she had with Jack was still too new, too private and too uncertain for public sharing.

Oh, and, by the way, Uncle Jonathan, would you mind not mentioning to my father that he has another daughter ready to plunge the family into scandal... ?

Jack looked at her, his slate blue eyes unreadable, and then at his father. "I'm just saying I don't trust the hotel to provide her with adequate protection, that's all."

Jonathan nodded. "So, we'll get her police protection."

"I can try to get a uniform assigned to her door," Martinez said. "But we've got an entire city to serve. The department's resources don't stretch to providing personal protection for visiting celebrities." His polite tone barely covered his scorn.

Norris stirred from his position by the food cart. "The team's available tonight, Senior, until 0900 tomorrow. We can put one man on the door and three outside the building to cover the access points and windows."

"Why the windows?" Christina inquired.

Jack hesitated.

"Snipers," Norris explained simply.

Fear froze her throat. She swallowed. "Oh."

"I don't think we need to worry about snipers," Martinez said. "This guy's an amateur. He missed a clear shot at fifty feet this afternoon."

"Anybody can miss at fifty feet with a twenty milli-meter handgun," Jack said.

"I wouldn't," Norris said under his breath.

Jack glared at him before turning back to the detective. "Besides, we don't know if he was acting alone."

"The detective has a point, son," Jonathan said. "We don't know for sure that Kamal's men are targeting the princess."

"Well, *somebody's* targeting her. And at this point I don't give a damn who. She can be killed by a kook as easily as by a terrorist."

Frustration rasped in his voice. Forgetting the roomful of observers, Christina laid a hand on his arm. He shrugged it off.

She curled her hand into a fist and laid it in her lap, hiding her hurt. No scenes.

Martinez leaned forward in his chair. "Do you have any idea why someone would want to kill you, Dr. Sebastiani?"

She rubbed her forehead wearily. "I told you. No."

"What about Cunningham?" Jack asked suddenly. He turned to his father. "Did you check him out?"

Martinez looked interested. "Who is this Cunningham?"

Jack shrugged. "An old boyfriend. From UCLA."

"Not in L.A. anymore," Jonathan said. "He's making independent films in North Carolina."

"But there could be someone else?" Martinez persisted. "A rival? A lover?"

The security expert stopped chewing to listen. Norris and the hotel manager looked at her with frank speculation in their eyes.

"I don't have lovers," Christina objected.

Jack turned his head, and her blood thrummed in her

ears. Well, all right, as of last night, she had a lover. And she wanted him back, damn it, wanted these men gone and her life in order again.

"Perhaps someone you slighted, then," Martinez suggested.

Jonathan clasped his hands behind his back. "According to my source in L.A., if we suspect every man the princess turned down in four years, you'd have to investigate half the campus."

Norris grinned.

Christina's nails dug into her palms. She hated this, hated being reduced to a royal *thing,* alternately shot at and sheltered, examined and ordered about.

"It doesn't matter," Jack said. "I'm taking her back to Montana. By private jet, if I can."

"I have my plane," his father volunteered.

The security expert returned to his sandwich. The hotel manager went back to watching TV. Norris sprawled, at ease and not at ease, his attention on Jack.

"I'd really prefer Dr. Sebastiani remain available until we have a suspect in custody," Martinez said smoothly. "In case she can identify him."

"And how are you going to make an arrest?" Jack demanded. "You don't have prints. You don't have witnesses. I'm not risking her neck while you hunt for leads."

Christina straightened her shoulders. "It's my neck," she said clearly. "If I can help with the investigation, Detective, then I am happy to cooperate."

"Forget it," Jack said.

Martinez ignored him. "Give me forty-eight hours," the detective urged Christina. "If we haven't turned up anyone in that time, then we're unlikely to make a quick arrest anyway and you can go."

"And in the meantime, she's defenseless," Jack growled.

Jonathan Dalton raised his eyebrows. "In the meantime, she has you."

"She has us," Norris said. "I'll have your film developed when I get back to the base, Senior. Those shots you took of the princess's talk? Maybe we'll get a lead from those. Like you said, you never know what will show up on camera."

"This is it," the hotel manager said suddenly.

Bewildered, Christina looked to Jack. He jerked his head toward the television as the camera panned the hotel lobby and lingered over a silent sound bite from Dr. Ungarro.

"For god's sake, turn up the volume," Jonathan ordered.

The security expert grabbed the remote and thumbed the control.

The shot cut to the newsroom. "...still searching for leads on her unknown assailant," the pretty brunette anchorwoman said.

"Is that it?" asked the hotel manager.

"That's not bad," Jonathan said.

"Be glad they didn't have footage of the shooting," Martinez said cynically.

The picture changed again, to a still color photograph.

And there was Christina, her kiss-reddened lips, her bed-tousled hair, her white skin showing between the panels of her whiter robe, framed in her hotel doorway. The photographer had caught Jack on the point of leaving her hotel room, and the picture left no doubt who was responsible for her tumbled state.

Christina went numb.

Ice cubes rattled at the bar as Jonathan Dalton set down his glass. The security man gulped his sandwich.

Norris whistled. "Like I said, you never know what will show up on camera."

The anchorwoman continued in an arch voice-over. "Isn't it nice to know that, despite the attack, Princess Christina is enjoying at least some of her stay in San Diego. Tune in to *Celebrity Grapevine* tonight at seven to learn more about this most reclusive member of Montebello's royal family."

"I know Sy Fuller over at the networks," Jonathan Dalton announced, running a hand through his thick white hair. "I'll see what I can do to get the story pulled."

Jack smiled bleakly. This time, it seemed, the old man was determined to come through. The minute Jack had called to report on the shooting, Jonathan had made plans to come to San Diego, made promises to pull strings.

It was impossible not to appreciate his father's instant support. Hard not to question his motives. And damn difficult not to be irritated by his familiar take-charge routine.

The police had left, the hotel manager and the head of hotel security had left, Bill Norris had left to develop Jack's film and call in the rest of the team, but the major, bless him, was still on the scene.

Only this time Jack wasn't a resentful sixteen-year-old boy coping with the loss of his mother. This time he was a man trying to protect the woman he loved.

He glanced at Christina, sitting straight and pale on one of the hotel's overupholstered chairs, resisting the drag of the down cushions. Her hands were folded in her lap to hide their trembling. Her chin was lifted. A thin red line from a falling shard of the shattered vase marred the perfection of her upper lip. She was beautiful, and so damn brave she made his heart ache.

Jack had seen courage under fire and after trauma before. No SEAL survived without it. But how many modern princesses had it? In the past seven hours, Christina had been shot at, questioned by the police and exposed on TV. But since he'd dragged her up off the hotel carpet and hustled her to her room, not one whimper, not one word of complaint, had escaped her.

That took more than class. It took guts.

"Or I might be able to get someone in the State Department to put pressure on them from the national security angle," Jonathan continued.

"I don't think one indiscreet photo of the princess constitutes a threat to United States security," Jack said dryly.

"Anything that destabilizes the ruling house of Montebello could affect American interests there. Not to mention that it's a distraction and a disappointment at a time when the king needs all his concentration to deal with Kamal."

Christina winced, so slightly that Jack almost missed the movement. "Does my father have to know?"

"If I don't tell him, he'll read about it in the tabloids. And with your brother presumed dead and your sister pregnant pregnant and Sheik Ahmed yelling conspiracy, the last thing your family needs is another scandal." Jonathan whirled on his son. "Damn it, Jack, I expected better from you."

"Did you?" Jack asked coolly. "That's a first."

His father looked away. "You shouldn't be in her hotel room."

"You're in her hotel room."

"That's different," Jonathan said.

Hell, he knew that. But he wouldn't let the old man embarrass Christina. "Why? I'm assigned to protect her."

"And this is how you do it? By exposing her to scandal? By undercutting her academic credibility?"

"He saved my life," Christina said.

"I let your shooter escape. You're still in danger, princess."

Her chin lifted. "Then I need your protection even more."

Her simple faith unnerved him. He didn't deserve it. He didn't deserve her. How could she not be scared? He was. He was terrified of losing her. Terrified of letting her down.

But as long as she depended on him, he could not walk away.

Jonathan Dalton looked from his firstborn son to the daughter of his friend, the king of Montebello. And for once it was hard for Jack to guess what the old man was thinking.

"Fine," he said. "Stay with her. But no more photos."

Chapter 16

The phone jerked Jack from his three-minute catnap. He lifted the receiver. "Dalton."

Merlin's tenor flowed warm and smooth over the line. "You know, Senior, this protection business would be a hell of a lot easier if we could treat it as a standard op. What do you say tomorrow I get in there and work a little communications magic? Radios, microphones, cameras…"

Jack fought to keep a grin from his voice. "Are you suggesting liberating government property for personal use, Johnson?" he asked severely.

"I would never do such a thing, Senior Chief." There was a two-beat pause. "Not over an unsecured line, anyway."

Jack laughed. God, it felt good to work with his team again. Good to be in action again, even though action, at this moment, was mostly sitting by the phone torturing himself with thoughts of Christina.

He knew what she looked like naked now. He didn't have to imagine the texture of her skin or the curve of her breasts or the gentle slope of her stomach. He didn't even have to close his eyes to see her strong, graceful body pale against the darkness. She was burned into his retinas like the afterglow of an explosion.

His smile faded. No, he didn't have to imagine her.

He had to stay away from her.

To protect her reputation, sure. But more, to protect his own soul. Because when all this was over, when the terrorists were caught and Christina of Montebello was back in her ivory tower, there could be no room in her dedicated, disciplined, privileged life for one washed-up former Navy SEAL.

"Senior?" Merlin's quiet voice pulled him back to the task at hand. "Little John reports the target is moving. The heat tracker shows her approaching an exit point. In fact, it looks like she—"

The connecting door between Jack's room and Christina's room opened, and she stood in the doorway, wearing a pale blue silky number that made her look like the queen of the fairies.

A very sexy queen of the fairies.

Jack nearly swallowed his tongue. "It's all right, Johnson. I've got the situation under control."

Sure he did.

"Hoo-yah, Senior." Was there a hint of laughter in the system tech's voice?

There was the faint click of the disconnect in Jack's ear, and then Merlin and his amusement didn't matter, nothing mattered, because Christina was moving across the room toward him, the pale blue silk flowing over her curves like water.

"You shouldn't be in here," Jack said bluntly.

She stopped at the foot of his bed. "Your door was unlocked."

God, she saw right through him.

"For security reasons," he said.

She arched a blond eyebrow. "I'm a scientist, Jack. I deal in facts. The fact is you could have that door unlocked in two seconds. The fact is, you didn't lock it. And since you didn't, I made the logical deduction that you wanted me in your room. Now, if I was wrong…" She shrugged, and the silk slithered on her shoulders and shimmered in the light of the bedside lamp.

"No," he said hoarsely. "I want you."

In his room. In his bed. In his life. His chest ached with wanting her.

But he couldn't tell her that, couldn't deliver some kind of emotional ultimatum while she still depended on him for her safety.

"But the *fact* is, we're a news item now," he said heavily. "There's a police officer and a Navy SEAL parked outside your door this very minute. So maybe what you should ask yourself is what do you want, princess? You want to risk it getting out that you're getting it on with your bodyguard?"

Her chin lifted. He loved her pride, loved the spark of temper in her eyes. "Maybe I want to thank you for saving my life."

"I get paid to save your life. I don't need you in my bed as some sort of good conduct prize."

"Then maybe I just want you."

His mouth went dry. Oh, boy. There was the kicker. What if she really did? Want him. Not the Texas hell-raiser or the Navy SEAL or the reluctant bodyguard, but him. Jack Dalton. Because if she ever did want him, the man he was inside, well, then he was damned if he could see how he could resist her.

"You heard the major. What about your family? What about your 'academic credibility'?"

"It's amazing how being shot at does wonders for your perspective." She smiled, and his breath caught. Her fingertips touched his chest. "Anyway, no one needs to know I'm here."

And his brief, pathetic fantasy blew up like an Iraqi munitions dump.

Sure, she wanted him. Wanted how he could make her feel when no one would know, where no one could see. Wanted him to provide an exciting little interlude in her purposeful, productive life.

But she didn't want to love him. Didn't want him to love her.

Because the real scandal would be the princess of Montebello wasting her life tangled up with an out-of-work warrior with a track record of failed relationships.

She looked up at him, her wonderful, clear blue eyes searching and uncertain. "Jack?"

Hell, how could he be angry with her? She was only playing the game by the rules he set. Sex without commitment. Without repercussions. He was some lucky bastard that she wanted to have it with him. Except for one pesky, unforeseen consequence.

He was in love with her.

No, he wasn't. He wouldn't let himself be. That wasn't how this game was won.

He pulled her to him, firmly, felt the surprise and then the give in her body as she settled against him. Her arms crept around his neck. Her yielding almost tricked him into slowing down, tempted him to hold her close for long, slow minutes and tell her how wonderful she was, how fine and smart and brave.

Only she hadn't come for words.

He palmed her breast, squeezing and releasing the soft flesh until the nipple hardened against his fingers, under the silk. He plucked at the tip, his mouth moving down to find and suckle her other breast.

Her hands fluttered on his shoulders. "Jack—" she said, in plea or protest.

He stopped her words with his mouth, with his tongue. He felt the resistance in her and drove through it, plunging deep, commanding her response. And when he had it, when her hands tightened and her lips clung and she was kissing him back, he raised his head and whispered against her wet lips, "Ssh. We've got an audience posted outside the door."

Awareness shivered through her. She nodded, and then she surprised him, standing on tiptoe to kiss him again, her lips soft and sweet. Understanding. Loving.

Not loving, he reminded himself harshly. But maybe, with her soft breasts flattened against his chest and her smooth arms wrapped around him, love didn't matter.

He pushed her legs apart with his thigh and ground against her, pelvis to pelvis, his hardness to her softness, his heat to her heat. And instead of pushing him away, she half closed her eyes and moved with him. He almost exploded. He slid his hands down and around and cupped her bottom, filling his palms with her, guiding her against him. The soft silk rubbed between them. It was almost better than having her naked. Almost.

Thank God there hadn't been time for Merlin to install his bugs and cameras in the room. Because Jack wanted Christina naked, and he wanted her now. Now, and for as many times as she would come to him.

He pulled at her slippery excuse for a nightgown without much caring if he ripped it. And maybe Christina didn't care, either, because her own hands were busy on his shirt and on the buckle of his belt. He lowered her onto the bed and came down on top of her, and her arms and legs wrapped around him, cradled him, made them one. He was breathing hard. She sighed.

He moved his hand between them, down her stomach, feeling the muscles contract, seeking the evidence of her arousal. Her hips bucked up, into him, but her hand touched his cheek, impossibly gentle, achingly tender.

"Jack," she whispered, "don't you think we should slow—"

"No," he said, and claimed her mouth again.

He used his body and his experience to overwhelm her, commanding her responses, undermining her slight reluctance. He kissed her, wet, deep kisses, and then he laced his fingers with hers and pinned her to the mattress and pushed, slowly, deeply, completely, into her. Her mouth was soft. Her eyes were open. She was all open to him, soft and pink and open, and she sighed and arched against him.

She was silk and fire, burning under him. He closed his heart to her and fed the heat with deliberate skill, felt the tension spiral in her body. This was what she wanted, wasn't it? This much he could give her. He pushed into her, feeling her stretch and contract around him, so hot, so tight, so wet, he almost lost his control. He set his jaw and braced his arms and moved faster, sliding into her, thrusting into her. He felt her struggle to keep up, and he pushed her, driving her, harder, faster now, driving them both past thought and into the dark. She writhed under him. Panting, he plunged into her, wringing her climax from her, taking his own. This was how the game was played. This was how the game was won.

So why, as his body collapsed on hers, as she shuddered silently under him and her hands stroked his wet back, did he feel like the world's biggest loser?

Christina stroked the short, damp hair at the back of Jack's neck as her pulse thrummed and her mind rattled and her heart broke slowly into a hundred pieces.

She felt like the spoiled princess in one of her mother's stories, the one who was given the stars and still whined for the moon. She had Jack's respect and his cautiously tendered friendship. He seemed determined to provide her with both protection and hot sex.

She couldn't blame him because she wanted more.

Their bodies were slick from their lovemaking. His weight pressed her into the mattress. She felt about a million miles away and all alone.

She stared up at the ceiling. Stupid. She'd accepted the rules of the game when she came to his room. It wasn't fair to him to change them now.

It wasn't his fault that she'd fallen in love with him.

Her throat constricted. She could not bind him. Her love would not let her. Her pride would not allow it. She knew what it was like to feel trapped by obligation. She'd grown up in the prison created by her family's expectations. She would die before…well, all right, that was awfully melodramatic. She was a scientist. She was pretty sure she would not die—but she simply could not inflict her own feelings on Jack as long as his honor trapped him to her side.

Before he had taken on her protection, he had traveled all over the world. He was drifting across the country. He was a warrior. A wanderer. She could not ask him to give up his freedom to stay with her.

There was a tap at the door. Jack's door. She felt him stiffen.

"What is it?" she whispered.

He lifted his head from her shoulder. "Could be Norris. I told him to report back if he found…" He levered his body away from hers, already gone from her in his mind. She almost wept at the loss.

He dressed with quick, efficient movements while she huddled under the sheet.

"You want to get back to your room?" he asked, tugging on his belt.

She clutched the covers. "Is he coming in?"

He gave her a brief, unreadable look. "That depends on what he's got."

She lifted her chin. She was not ashamed of being Jack's lover. But she wasn't going to sit here naked in his bed while he and his SEAL buddy discussed the attempt on her life. "I'll go get dressed," she said.

Tugging her blue negligee and her dignity around her, she escaped.

She armored herself in slacks and a silk blouse before she tapped lightly on the connecting door and admitted herself back into the room.

She narrowed her eyes. All the lights were on. Jack was sitting with Norris at the room's one table. He had jerked the spread up over the bed, and black-and-white photos covered both surfaces.

The two men were speaking in lowered voices, but she could hear the excitement humming under the surface. All talk stopped at her entrance.

She stopped, too, feeling awkward and out of place.

She was so damn pretty, Jack thought, fear and lust and pride in her momentarily striking him dumb.

Her slacks and blouse were ironed and elegant. She'd reapplied her makeup and done something simple and sophisticated to her hair so that it coiled neatly on her neck. But nothing could disguise the soft flush of her skin or that kiss-bruised mouth. She exuded sex—sex over ice, he'd described her once, and that was when she wasn't fresh from his bed.

He groaned silently. In a matter of hours, the entire squad would have confirmation that Jumpin' Jack Flash was getting it on with royalty.

Horse grinned his appreciation and stood. "Ma'am."

She smiled hesitantly. "Mr. Norris."

"Sit down, Norris," Jack snapped. "We have work to do."

"Yes, Senior Chief," Norris said respectfully.

Jack wasn't fooled into thinking he'd heard the last about his association with the princess. But he had more serious worries right now. "Make an enlargement of this one," he ordered. "And copies. We'll need copies. Run them by the hotel staff, see if anybody can identify—"

Christina took a step forward. "Who? What are you talking about?"

It was her life. She deserved to know what was going on. Jack pulled his chair out for her to sit at the table. "I think we've found your shooter."

She looked at him over her shoulder as he pushed in the chair. "How? Where?"

He checked his own excitement. He hadn't saved her yet. "In the pictures I took of your workshop. Here." His finger tapped a photograph on the table. "The skinny guy in the beard. Take off the glasses and add a red hat, and we've got the man who shot at you."

She bent her head to look. Her brows drew together as she studied the photograph. "No."

"What do you mean, no?"

"There must be some other explanation. I know this man."

Norris stirred. "Begging your pardon, ma'am, but—"

"How?" Jack asked.

"He's from UCLA. He was a fellow in disease studies there when I was an undergraduate."

"Do you remember his name?"

She nodded. "Omer. Sinan Omer."

Norris snorted. "He sure doesn't sound like he's from around Los Angeles."

"Well, he's not from Tamir, either," Christina said in her clipped, precise way. "His family came from Yemen, I think. Or Maloun? But being an Arab doesn't make him a terrorist."

"Whoever, whatever he is, he shot at you," Jack said.

Her face closed in instinctive rejection. "No. I *know* him."

"I hate to break it to you, princess, but most victims are murdered by people they know. It's only in war that you have the luxury of being killed by strangers."

"Was he, like, a boyfriend or something?" Norris asked.

Her face turned pink, but she answered him steadily. "No. He was older. Seven or eight years, I think. He asked me out once, but I told him I didn't date within the department. And after that he didn't pay any attention to me at all."

She didn't have a clue, Jack thought. He may have taken her virginity, but he hadn't touched her fundamental innocence. She had no idea how that come-and-get-me body and touch-me-not air could mess with a man's mind.

She'd probably thought she was being friendly when she'd slapped this Omer character down. She wouldn't grasp that a man could look at her and hunger, how it could chafe his pride and soul to realize that that cool perfection was forever out of reach.

She didn't understand how it twisted a man's gut to be offered her quick intelligence and dry humor and warm affection—even her presence in his bed—when what he wanted was her soul.

But Jack did. Oh, yeah, he understood that all too well.

"Run a check," he told Norris.

"But—" Christina almost sputtered. "He's head of the visiting speakers program at UCLA. Dr. Kauffman— Marty—was going to tell him to call me."

Norris looked at Jack. "Professional jealousy, you think?"

Jack shrugged. "Might have been a trigger. See what else you can dig up. I'm going to Martinez with what we've got. I want this son of a bitch locked up."

"Arrested?" Jonathan Dalton waved the waiter away. Father and son were eating lunch at the hotel's best restaurant. Jonathan could afford the best, and Jack wanted this conversation to take place where Christina wouldn't overhear. "When?"

"Four hours ago. Martinez called me." Jack rubbed the knot of tension at the back of his neck. "They're waiting for the judge to set bond."

"They won't release him," Jonathan said confidently. "The United States government does not want some terrorist wandering around taking potshots at the princess of Montebello."

Jack's headache got worse. "We haven't established that he is a terrorist. He's a respected academic with no priors. Without an active link to a known terrorist organization, it's going to be tough to convince the judge that one skinny, obsessed biology professor with bad aim is a danger to the community.''

"What if he confesses?"

"He's already confessed. To sending the note, and to firing the shot. But Martinez warned me that the court might take that as a sign that Omer is prepared to cooperate. Our best hope is to convince the judge that he's a flight risk.''

Jonathan snorted and dug into his steak. "A flight risk? Where's he going to go? The teacher's lounge?"

"Maloun.''

Jonathan lowered his knife. "Explain," he ordered his son.

Jack pushed his own plate out of the way and leaned forward across the heavy linen tablecloth. "I had Norris run a background check on this guy. He's clean. No suspicious activities at all. But it turns out his father was part of the rebellion against Marcus before the king even took the throne.''

"When he was crown prince," Jonathan said. "I remember. That's when I got to know Marcus, as part of his peacemaking force.''

Of course. But then, his father had hired himself out to a lot of causes in his long years as a mercenary.

Jack continued. "Anyway, when Marcus put down the uprising, it forced Omer Senior to the States. He went from being a hotshot intellectual leader in his homeland to working menial jobs in the L.A. public schools. According to Norris's report, he eventually settled down, even married an American woman. But apparently he raised a son with strong academic ambitions and a grudge against the Sebastianis.''

Jonathan nodded. "Which made Sinan Omer an excellent tool in Sheik Ahmed's feud against Montebello."

Jack cleared his throat. He was taking a risk here. Going out on a limb. The major had hired him as a royal baby-sitter, not as a conspiracy consultant. "Actually, I don't think it did."

Jonathan frowned. "But you just finished telling me—"

"Omer's motivation for attacking Christina, yeah. He had reasons to want her dead. Jealous bastard reasons, but reasons. Kamal doesn't."

Instead of blowing up at him, the major looked thoughtful. "How do you figure that? Marcus is convinced Sheik Ahmed is behind the threats to his family. The attack on Julia—"

"—was a kidnap attempt. And sure, Kamal had good reasons for that. With the prince missing, Julia is the heir, right? Not to mention that she's pregnant with the sheik's grandchild. Holding Julia would give him control over the Montebellan succession. But what motive does Kamal have for killing Christina? Christina's no threat to him. She's not even in line for the throne."

"What motive does he need? The two houses have been feuding for over a hundred years."

"But they've never resorted to murder."

The major shifted his silverware around on the table-cloth. "I don't know, Jack. Ahmed believes Marcus is somehow responsible for Sheik Rashid's disappearance. Maybe he wants revenge."

"Is that what he says?"

"No," Jonathan admitted. "Kamal still claims he's innocent."

"So, it's his word against the king's suspicions."

The major stopped fussing with the flatware. "Yes. And

my loyalty and my interests lie with Marcus. As do yours.''

"My loyalty lies with Christina," Jack said steadily. "And that means finding out if she's still in any danger. Maybe Omer acted alone. Maybe he didn't. We need to find out."

"How?"

"Princess Julia is your primary target. Why not use her to draw whoever was behind the kidnap attempt into the open?"

"Jack, for God's sake, she's pregnant. The king would never permit it."

"Then get an agent to stand in for her. A look-alike."

His father frowned thoughtfully. "Whoever we find will still need protection."

At least the old man hadn't tossed the idea out immediately. Jack let out his breath. "Of course."

Jonathan raised his eyebrows. "Are you interested?"

"In what?" Jack asked cautiously.

"Guarding our decoy until we determine who was behind the attacks."

Jack went very still. God, he was tempted. But… "I can't leave Christina until this is settled. You'll have to find somebody else."

"I can do that, of course," Jonathan said slowly. "Do you remember Caleb Stone? I've worked with him for a number of years."

Jack narrowed his eyes. Where was the old man going with this? He never discussed his work with Jack. "Not really," he said.

"I suppose it doesn't matter. I was just thinking of his son, Hawk. Hawk's a police officer, a fine one. We could bring him in to guard our decoy princess. But you did an excellent job on this assignment, son. I hate to lose you."

Jack forced himself to smile. "Offering me a job, Dad?"

"Not really a job. More of a...calling," his father said unexpectedly. "Have you ever heard of a group called the Noble Men?"

Jack frowned. "It's a covert military organization, isn't it? One of my instructors at Coronado was really stuck on them, so we heard a lot about them—rescues, medical ops, saving the occasional small monarchy. The lieutenant couldn't decide if they were peace brokers or lawbreakers. He did tell our class that the so-called Noble Men didn't have to follow the restrictions imposed by a civilian government."

Jonathan stiffened. "We prefer to think of ourselves as having the power to step in to alleviate injustice where governments can't."

Jack felt his jaw drop level with the pristine white tablecloth. "'We'? You're one of them?"

"It's worse than that," his father said dryly. "I organized them."

Chapter 17

The dining room whirled and fell into place again with a clink of silverware and a woman's laugh.

Jack focused on his father, sitting soldier straight and statesman serious on the other side of the table, as if he hadn't just lobbed a conversational grenade in the middle of his sixteen-ounce rib steak.

"You organized the Noble Men," Jack repeated.

It was incredible. And at the same time, it explained a lot: the absences and evasions, the calls from kings and cabinet members, his family's wealth and his mother's loneliness.

Jonathan inclined his head. "I pulled together the original five. Men I trusted. Men I served with in Nam. Cal Stone was one. We were all out of the services by then, doing similar work for hire. Combining our abilities, our resources, gave us more choices over the jobs we selected—and more power to accomplish our aims."

"What aims?" Jack asked skeptically. More money? More power?

"All of us had seen enough war to know it's the innocent who suffer most. We threw our lot in where we thought we could change that."

"Without answering to any government."

Jonathan's eyes narrowed. "We answer to ourselves. To each other, and to our sense of honor. On the whole, it's a policy that has served us—and the world—well."

"Then why the hell didn't you tell me? Why let me think your services were for sale to the highest bidder?"

"I didn't want to put you at risk by involving you in my cause," Jonathan explained. "I wanted you to have the chance for a normal life, with a home and family."

Jack set his jaw. "I didn't think that was important to you."

"I tried to make it important. I guess I just wasn't cut out to be a family man." Jonathan smiled wryly. "I guess even when I was ready to try again, after your mother died, I proved I wasn't a very good father."

Hell. Jack so did not want to get into a game of truth or consequences right now.

"You were good with Janey," he said, giving the old man his due. Maybe that would satisfy him.

"I was less successful with you. When I came home, you were so much the man already, I forgot you were also a sixteen-year-old boy. My sixteen-year-old boy. I gave you orders when I should have given you my time."

Okay, so it was going to be truth or consequences, after all. And Jack wasn't going to lose this game, either.

"Time would have been good. Or I might have settled for the truth. Like, 'Hey, kid, sorry I wasn't here for your mother's funeral, but I was off saving the world.' I would have accepted that, you know. As an excuse, it beats the hell out of 'I was sticking up foreign dictators for another five grand.'"

The major looked shaken. "I didn't know. I thought it was in your best interests to keep you out of that part of my life."

"So why drag me into it now? Why hire me instead of one of your other stooges?"

"For the same reason, I suppose."

"My best interests?" Jack said warily.

"Yes. Son... Maybe we're more alike than either one of us ever wanted to acknowledge. I didn't interfere in your life as long as you were in the SEALs. But when you left the navy—"

"You mean, when I started bumming around the country?"

"You used to have pride, Jack. You had purpose."

"And you thought this job would give them back to me."

Jonathan nodded. "I hoped the organization would, yes. Our work certainly has provided me with both for many years. But even if the Noble Men didn't give you back that pride and purpose, I thought Christina might."

Jack scowled. Did his father think one simple assignment could replace his life on the Teams? Or was he playing matchmaker? Neither one sat well.

"So, you hired me as—what? Some kind of therapy?"

"No. I hired you because you were the best man available for the job."

It was a level of involvement Jack had never expected from the major. And a level of trust he'd never had.

"Right. And what about Christina? What if she'd been abducted? Or killed? Don't you think it was a little irresponsible to put her life at risk so that I could get back my sense of pride and purpose?"

"Nonsense," the major said sharply. "I knew you would protect Christina. And you've succeeded beyond my expectations—not only saved her life, but identified and apprehended her shooter. As well as giving us something to think about regarding Sheik Ahmed. Which is why—" Jonathan leaned forward in his chair and regarded his son closely "—I'm prepared to offer you the responsibility of serving as operations consultant to the Noble Men."

Jack took a short, sharp breath. "What does that mean?"

"Our organization maintains teams to send on missions—just as the SEALS do. You would coordinate and advise them."

"You mean, go into the field?"

"As needed. That would be up to you."

The possibility lit up his dreary prospects like Tomahawk missiles over the desert. It was everything Jack had once wanted. Action. Adventure. Employment.

"I couldn't start until I know Christina's safe," he said steadily.

Jonathan raised his eyebrows. "And then what? Judging from what I saw on the news the other night—"

"It's not—you can't believe everything you see on TV."

"You disappoint me," the major said.

"Not for the first time."

His father didn't smile.

Jack crumpled his napkin in frustration and tossed it on the table. "Oh, come on, Dad. It would never work. She's a princess. And I'm hardly a prince. Or even a knight in shining armor."

"You're my son. My heir. And the king is my friend."

Jack shook his head stubbornly. "I'm not what she needs."

"Which is what?"

"Someone who can fit into her life in Montana. Someone who will be there for her."

"Like I wasn't there for your mother," Jonathan guessed.

Jack was silent.

The major sighed. "You know, this position with the Noble Men...you'll have the freedom to pick and choose which missions you oversee personally."

"That doesn't change the fact that I could leave her pregnant and alone. Like my mother, yes. Or like her sister. You were right, Dad. We're too much alike for me to think I'd make a good husband."

"I think you're forgetting something important," Jonathan said.

"What's that?"

"You're not me. And Christina is not your mother. She's a strong woman, with a strong mind of her own. If she's decided she wants you—"

"Well, she doesn't," Jack said shortly. "So that problem's eliminated."

The major frowned. "Except for the scandal."

"Leave the scandal to me," Jack said. "I have an idea."

"You cannot be serious." Christina stopped folding her conference blazer—peacock-blue Armani—to stare at Jack, handsome and lean and stubborn in the doorway of her bedroom. "I don't do interviews."

"You didn't do interviews," he said. "You should now."

Pure funk made her hands shake. She couldn't possibly. Didn't he see that? "You were the one who wanted me to make a quick exit to Montana."

"I still do. Eliza Windmere from the print media and

Jeri Stone and the *Celebrity Grapevine* camera crew are scheduled for this afternoon at two. You can give them a couple of hours and still make it to the airport tonight.''

Celebrity Grapevine. Her stomach lurched. ''But your father's pilot—''

''—will wait.''

Deprived of excuses, she fell back on refusal. Bending over the bed, she jerked her jacket into a rough rectangle. ''I won't do it.''

''I thought you were done with running away,'' he goaded her softly.

She stopped fussing with the blazer to glare at him. ''I am not giving the media more ammunition to use against my family.''

''You wouldn't be. You've let them define you long enough. It's time you let the world see who you really are. We control the setting, you control the image.'' He left the doorway, strolled forward. ''I spoke to Stone. In return for feature coverage, she's promised a cream puff interview.''

Christina bit her lower lip. ''What if she asks about us?''

Jack shrugged. ''Tell the truth.''

Her heart leaped into her throat. She swallowed. ''What is the truth?''

He met her gaze. His eyes were bleak and blue. ''There is no 'us,''' he said deliberately.

His words lanced her. She knew that. She was expecting it, really. But, oh, it hurt.

''Thank you for making that perfectly clear,'' she said. Very cool. Very dignified. Her mother would have been proud.

Jack winced. ''It's not that you're not a great person,'' he began.

She forgot about dignity. ''Oh, spare me,'' she snapped.

"I am not one of those girls you pick up in a bar and have to ease out the door the next morning. I do not need a speech about what a wonderful person I am. I know my value. I know who I am and I know what I have to offer. I could give you a mind to laugh with and a heart to love with and a warm, willing body in your bed at night. I could give you a home and a family. And if you don't want them—if you don't want me—that's your loss."

His jaw tightened.

Good, she thought nastily. Why should she be the only miserable one?

"You know I want you," he rasped.

"You want my body." She flung the words back at him.

"I want all of you, damn you." He grabbed her shoulders and hauled her close. His breath was hot. His face was furious. "But I don't have the right to ask."

"For pity's sake, why not?"

"I'm not what you need."

He was so close, she thought despairingly. Surely she could reach him? With her words, with her touch, with her love.

"You might let me be the judge of that," she said.

Jack's grip bruised her shoulders. "You don't have the experience to judge. I do. I've seen what happens to a marriage when a man is gone all the time. What happens to a woman. I've seen it with my mother. I've seen it in the SEALs."

She was confused. "But you're not a SEAL anymore."

"Not quite." His hands released her. "I've accepted a job with my father, Christina."

She arched an eyebrow. "Global Enterprises?"

He laughed shortly. "Global peace is more like it. He's one of the Noble Men, Christina. That's his connection with your father. That's why he hired me to look after you. I've accepted his offer to serve as operations consultant for his mercenary force, and that—'' he drew a deep breath ''—that's why I can't stay with you.''

Her heart, her face, her lips were numb. It was too much to take in. ''When are you leaving?'' she asked stiffly.

''Not until this business with Kamal is resolved. When I know for certain that you're safe.''

She hadn't lost him. Yet. She moistened her dry lips with her tongue. ''I could—''

''No,'' he interrupted harshly. ''You couldn't. I'd be gone, Christina. Not all the time, but often enough. I can't ask you to live with the fact that I'd be in danger, and you'd be alone.''

She lifted her chin. ''More alone than I'll be if you don't ask me?''

His face closed. ''I'll never ask you.''

The reporter, Eliza Windmere, was thin, red-haired and awkward. The *Celebrity* host, Jeri Stone, was sleek, dark and glamorous.

Jack had watched Christina welcome them both to her hotel suite with a grace that didn't quite disguise her reluctance or her nerves. She'd sat patiently while various flunkies fiddled with her makeup and the lighting, listened to a list of instructions from a diva with a clipboard and responded with a wan smile to a joke from the camera crew.

''It must be difficult living so far from home.'' Jeri leaned forward sympathetically in the green hotel chair, pointing her toe to emphasize the long line of her famous legs. ''Do you miss your family in Montebello?''

''Oh, yes,'' Christina said, smiling ruefully for the cameras. "My mother in particular. But of course my work here…"

She was in lecture mode, Jack thought from his post on one side of the room. Cool, dry, confident of her facts.

She didn't once look at him.

He didn't want her to. The less attention he attracted, the better for her. And the sooner she accepted that he had nothing to offer her, the better for both of them.

But he could watch her. Oh, yeah. Watch her and want her and wish that things could be different—that *he* could be different—for her.

He became aware that Jeri Stone had shifted in her chair, subtly changing her posture and the tone of the interview. "…sure that you were terrified by the recent attack. Can you tell us what you were thinking?"

He stiffened. But Christina only smiled again and shook her head. "I'm afraid I wasn't thinking much of anything. I mean, there I was, lying on the lobby carpet, with water dripping on my head and my bodyguard yelling at me to get down…"

She spun the story until it sparkled, making light of her danger and her fear. Her face was matte perfect under the hot lights. Why wasn't she sweating? Jack wondered. He was.

Jeri tapped a toe in disappointment. "You were very brave," she said.

"Oh," Christina said lightly. "I've been braver since."

"Your bodyguard," Jeri said. "Now, would that be—"

"Who was the man photographed outside your hotel room, your highness?" Eliza Windmere called from off camera.

"That was my bodyguard. Jack Dalton." Christina's smile widened as she looked directly into the camera. "The man I plan to marry."

* * *

"Are you out of your Phi Beta Kappa mind? What the hell possessed you, to come out with that on national TV?"

Jack's pacing brought him up against the hotel room's closet. He pivoted and strode back toward her, his hands jammed in his pockets, his face lean and hard and dangerous.

Christina's heart beat wildly in her throat. "You didn't have to say yes," she pointed out reasonably.

He stopped in front of her. "Oh, yeah, when the cameraman turned on me, I just should have shook my head and said 'Sorry, folks, this is just some dumb charade to keep the Sebastiani name out of the tabloids.'"

Her heart sank back down from her throat to her Feragamo pumps. "Is that what you thought?" she asked quietly.

"What am I supposed to think?" he demanded. He turned and prowled away from her again, to the velvet draped windows. "It won't work, you know," he said, looking down on the view of the harbor, washed by evening light. "Everybody's going to want to talk to you now. *Newsweek. People. Bride Magazine.*"

She firmed her chin. She absolutely was not going to cry. "Good. Maybe after they do a photo spread of my wedding dress you'll accept that I'm serious."

"Christina." His voice was deep and shaken. He turned to face her. With his body silhouetted against the tall windows, she could not see his expression. "You don't have to do this. You were doing great in that interview. You can't let a couple of reporters manipulate you into—"

"No one manipulated me into anything, all right?" She dropped her head, defeated, and stared at her hands. "It was all my own stupid idea."

She didn't even hear him cross the room, he moved so silently. His feet, in boots, and then his legs, in jeans, moved into her field of vision just beyond the span of her lap.

"Then...why?" he asked.

She twisted her fingers together in her lap. "You told me not to let myself be defined by how other people saw me. Not to accept their limits. But you were defining me, too, Jack. Defining us. The princess in the tower who can't bear to watch her knight ride off to war, isn't that it? Something like that, anyway."

She took a deep breath and raised her head. Her chest hurt. Her voice shook. "Well, I'm not going to let you limit me anymore. Not when you're the one person who made it possible for me to accept myself for who I really am."

He knelt on the carpet beside her chair. He took her hands in his. Big hands, she thought. Strong, safe hands. "Who are you, Christina?" he whispered.

And she gave herself into his keeping.

"You know who I am," she said. "I'm everything you told me I could be. Princess Christina of Montebello. And Dr. Sebastiani, too. And, most of all, the woman who loves you."

"I'm no good for you," he muttered.

"Oh, Jack." Her heart nearly broke with tenderness. "How can you see me so clearly and still be so blind to your true character?" She struggled for proof to make him see. "Jack." She sat up, her hands tightening on his. "Jack, what are you doing when we get back to Montana?"

He frowned. "Doing?"

"Yes. After you deliver me back to Billings, what then?"

He frowned. "I'm going to stay with you until we know who's behind the threats to your family."

"What about Sinan Omer?"

"Martinez took him into custody."

"All right, then, what about the offer from your father?"

"He's going to have to wait. You come first. I'm not going anywhere until I know for sure you're safe."

She arched her eyebrows. "Really? I come first?"

Irritation narrowed his eyes. "Of course you—" She waited for realization to dawn. She didn't wait long. The man she loved was stubborn, not stupid.

A corner of his mouth turned up in appreciation. "Cupcake," Jack said solemnly, "you are a dangerous and determined woman."

She grinned, satisfied. "Yes. I am."

"I won't always be in the field," he told her.

"I know."

"If I'm consulting, I can be based anywhere. Including Montana."

Her heart soared. "I'm glad to hear it."

"Once this business with Kamal is settled, we can go visit your family in Montebello. It would give you a chance to look at the mines, and me the opportunity to observe one of the Noble Men's training programs."

"That sounds convenient."

Jack rubbed his jaw. "There's only one detail unaccounted for."

Doubt pinched her. "What?"

His face set. "I've got to ask you to marry me."

Her breath hitched. "You—you don't have to. You already agreed to marry me in front of five million viewers."

"No, I have to. And since I'm on my knees already..." He held her hands. He met her eyes, his slate-blue gaze so warm and real and steady that she knew he was seeing all the way to her soul.

"I love you," he said seriously. "Will you be my home? Will you make a family with me?"

And her heart flooded with a lifetime of happily ever after.

"You are my home, Jack." She pulled his head close. "And I'm willing to get started on the family whenever you are."

"No time like the present," Jack said against her mouth. And kissed her.

A long breathless while later she said, "But your father's plane is waiting."

"Let it wait." Jack drew her down with him to the floor. Laughter and desire roughened his voice. "I told you, you come first."

* * * * *

Next month, look for

BORN BRAVE

by Ruth Wind

as Intimate Moments' riveting
FIRSTBORN SONS
series continues.

Turn the page for a sneak preview....

Chapter 1

Laurie Lewis was alone in the administrative offices of the FBI. She'd just finished arranging secondary cover for an agent who had just had to flee an assignment and had until moments ago been huddled in a bistro in Paris, looking for a way back to safety.

She stretched, wondering with a little ache of longing what it would be like to be out there, in a dark Paris bistro, waiting for a lifeline. Or better yet, what it would be like to pull off an assignment and maybe save a life or even a country.

Beyond the windows, a heavy spring rain poured out of dark sky, exaggerating the taillights of the cars in the streets and giving the whole, gardenlike section of the city a thick wash of green. Around her in the office, other administrative personnel like herself answered phones and questions, some mundane, some dull, some exciting bits like the one she'd just completed. Her specialty was identities and itineraries.

"Ms. Lewis, do you have a moment?"

Tugged from her reverie, Laurie looked up to see Timothy Lake, her immediate superior. "Sure, Mr. Lake."

She followed him down a hushed and carpeted hallway. He stopped at a conference room door, knocked briefly and ushered her inside. The vast, windowless room was furnished with a long mahogany table, various electronic equipment and a wall of television screens flickering with several different scenes. The table was flanked with three or four of the highest ranking members of the organization, along with a few others she didn't recognize. All of them wore the conservative suits that made up Washington business attire.

All but one. Sitting apart from the others was a man she assumed must be an agent. He wore a pair of well-worn jeans and a red corduroy shirt that brought out the glossy darkness of his shoulder length hair. He stared directly at Laurie with a measuring, serious expression that was not particularly friendly. His eyes were a vivid green, startling in the dark, Native American face.

"Gentlemen," said Mr. Lake, "this is Laurie Lewis."

A dark-haired man in his fifties was the first to speak. "Remarkable."

Another man, one Laurie recognized as Caleb Stone, who had been her liaison on a developing case in the Mediterranean, stood and extended his hand. Stone was an expert on the country of Montebello and had been working with Laurie for the past month on a project documenting the royal family. "Please sit down, Ms. Lewis. We have a matter of some urgency to discuss with you."

She took the chair he pulled out for her, uncomfortably aware of the scrutiny and low murmurs of some of the others. What was going on?

"Ladies and gentlemen," Mr. Stone said, "Ms. Lewis

has been a key research specialist for our agents dealing with the Montebello-Tamir situation. She put together the original research documents for our agents, and has written more than a dozen briefs. Ms. Lewis, will you tell the others what some of those briefs covered?"

"Of course." Aloud, she listed some of the more important dossiers she'd logged, and the three undercover operations she'd helped to arrange. She was proud of her work on it. "I would say I'm one of three or four experts on the Sebastiani history."

Stone smiled. "So you are, then, quite familiar with the habits of Princess Julia?"

"Of course. She recently confessed to being pregnant with Sheik Rashid Kamal's child." Laurie had been moved by the young princess's story. "And there are some rumors that she's missing, which is leading to even more volatility in the area."

"Ms. Lewis," said the first man who'd spoken. "Please look at the screen."

A picture of Princess Julia, obviously at a charity function of some sort, was called up on one of the monitors, showing a tall, slim woman with thick dark hair and milk-smooth skin. Her suit, an ecru linen, had likely cost half Laurie's monthly salary, and the Italian leather pumps she wore would likely have consumed the other half. "That was taken in London two and a half years ago, I believe," Laurie said.

"Yes." The man zoomed in on Princess Julia's face, a remarkably clear focus. "Now please look at this."

The second picture was one of Laurie in a beige wool suit she'd found for a song in the bargain basement of Saks, a suit she thought looked great on her. The man zoomed in on her face, and Laurie suddenly saw what she was meant to see. "Wow. Quite a resemblance," she said

ying to cover the sudden rush of excitement that
u through her. "I never noticed before."

"It's not just a resemblance," said Caleb Stone. "It's
uncanny. We've been over dozens of tapes, and you've
been under observation for several weeks. Your body
movements are much more American and athletic, and
your hair is lighter and longer than hers, but the facial
resemblance is truly remarkable."

"And?" she asked as coolly as possible.

"According to your file, you passed your field training
with the highest marks in the class. You're certified for
weapons and undercover work, and have recently been
listed for a commendation. Is that all correct?"

"Yes, sir." She folded her hands, discovered her fingers
were ice-cold. Her heart was beating so loudly she was
afraid they might hear it and think she was not at all capable of what they were obviously leading up to.

A silence fell. The pictures of the princess and Laurie
hung side by side in mute testimony, and everyone gathered looked at them without comment for a long moment.
Nervously, Laurie glanced toward the agent type against
the wall and found that he was regarding her again with
the same impassive, slightly hostile gaze. She scowled at
him. Did he think she couldn't impersonate the princess?

There were obviously those with doubts. She saw it in
their eyes—most especially in the eyes of those who knew
her. They *didn't* think she could do it. Three times in the
past year she'd been passed over for an entry-level field
position.

Feeling the disapproval gathering among her superiors,
Laurie had a sudden inspiration.

She plucked a pencil from the table and walked her
strong, American, tomboyish walk to the front of the room.
Tucking the pencil between her teeth, she twisted her hair

into a knot and secured it with the pencil, then unbuttoned
her suit jacket and tossed it over a chair.

At the front of the room, she turned her back and took
a long deep breath, using the time to pull in the details of
Princess Julia. She straightened her spine imperceptibly,
smoothed her skirt over her hips and then tugged slightly
on her silk tank top to show a hint more cleavage.

She turned around and, imagining a basket of fruit bal-
anced precariously on the top of her head, walked to the
microphone. In a soft, accented and throatier voice than
she ordinarily owned, she said, "On behalf of my father
and my country, I am so pleased to be here today." She
flashed the slightly trembling, elusive smile that was such
a trademark of the princess, a smile that intrigued millions,
and knew immediately that her gift for mimicry had allowed her to capture it perfectly.

The response was immediate—a laugh, then a quick
flurry of clapping. Only the agent on the sidelines seemed
unimpressed. Laurie inwardly rolled her eyes. She didn't
need his approval.

"I'd say we've found our operative," Caleb said.
"Hawk, will you come up here? Laurie, I'd like you to
meet my son, Hawk Stone. He'll be posing as your bodyguard."

Oh, great. Laurie struggled to keep her expression neutral as the man got to his feet and walked up to where they
stood. He moved with the alert reserve she associated with
animals in the wild, a wariness around his eyes that
showed nothing, a readiness in the shoulders. She had the
definite sense that he disapproved of her.

But she wasn't *about* to let this man get under her skin!